DEAD

FOR THE

SHOW

A Dead Detective Mystery

by

PEG HERRING

From Gwendolyn Press

Chapter One

"LOOK, LADY. YOU'RE DEAD. YOU MIGHT AS WELL FACE IT."

"*You* look, *mister*! I'm not falling for your stupid joke, so get out of my face!"

Chewing his lip, Seamus tried to stay calm. Mike had warned him about Cassie Parker, but her outburst, so unseemly that those nearby stared in open-mouthed astonishment, made his neck feel warm and his ears redden. How was he supposed to find out how the girl died if she refused to believe she was dead?

He should have chosen a less public place than the deck of what everyone simply called "the ship." Cassie's arms were folded in a classic posture of denial, and her fingers dug into her skin till the knuckles were white. While everyone else at the rail stood facing outward, she'd turned her back to the stunning view, staring instead at the ship's dull-gray wall, eyes glazed, mind obviously abuzz with dark thoughts.

Earlier that morning Miss Parker's counselor, a serene angel named Nancy, had told Cassie as gently as possible that she was dead. The meeting had been dignified and private, but Cassie's response hadn't been the usual tears and regrets. She'd told Nancy flatly that she didn't believe she was dead and never would.

A guest's refusal to accept death complicated matters for those in charge. How could they ask Cassie to decide her future if she refused to face reality? When Cassie stalked out of the office, Nancy had contacted Gabe, who'd talked to Michael, the angel in charge of client services, who'd sent Seamus, a dead detective, to offer to help Cassie understand her death.

Seamus was a cross-back, one who investigated suspicious deaths to give clients the closure they needed to move on. Though death was a fact, some of the dead didn't know why they'd died or at whose hand. Seamus was willing to return to life and find out how Cassie Parker, at the tender age of twenty-five, had died without any idea how it happened, or even that it had.

It had been a while since he'd had a client, and Seamus was bored, as usual, by the idyllic but monotonous conditions on the ship. As a result, he'd been anxious to meet Cassie and get the details of the job. He'd handled it badly, explaining who he was before she was ready to listen, which raised Miss Parker's hackles.

He'd tried to be subtle, but Seamus wasn't much for small talk. "Pretty, isn't it?" He'd said when he joined her at the rail. He gestured at the soft-colored void before them, so far beyond *pretty* that words couldn't capture it.

Cassie didn't answer, so he'd tried again. "It's kinda like watching a waterfall or a fire burning, you know? I lose all sense of time."

She waved an angry hand over her shoulder. "That, I would guess, is pyrotechnics, along with a mild hallucinogen piped into the staterooms. The rest is a matter of hiring con artists like you to play the roles. The question is why."

"Miss Parker, I'm—"

"—An actor sent to convince me I'm dead. Just save your breath, okay?"

Seamus had squared his shoulders, standing a little taller so he was almost eye to eye with her. "No, miss. I'm a detective. Gabe, the angel in charge, told Mike—"

An index finger approached his nose in a gesture that was almost violent. "I don't know Gabe or Mike, but I'll tell you what I told Nancy, who's no angel, either. I'm not dead, and you people will never convince me I am."

That was when Seamus had abandoned tact in favor of facts and was rewarded with an order from Cassie to get out of her face. Shifting his shoulders inside his pin-striped suit jacket, he tried once more. "Doesn't this place feel different to you, kind of unreal?"

"No!" she said a little too vehemently. "I feel fine. Not sick, not hurt. Alive."

He shook his head. "Don't you get that stuff here is impossible? The clothes, the anything-you-want meals, the entertainment, all perfect? Life was never like that."

"It's reality TV." She ran a hand through her short hair, tousling curls that immediately returned to order. "Or maybe you guys injected me with something."

He understood her confusion. Everything here felt real: the ship, the crew, even the bodies they were provided to ease them through the transition.

"Why would they drug you?" he asked.

Cassie rubbed at her nose with an abrupt gesture. "I don't

know. That's what's so stupid about this. There's no reason to—" Her voice broke. She was near tears, from fear or anger or both. "I was at work, at a completely safe place, and then I was here." She stood upright, and one hand extended toward Seamus in an almost pleading gesture before she pulled it back. Her lips tightened, and her final sentence came through her teeth. "I'm not dead, and I'm not saying another word until someone here admits that."

Cassie returned to staring at nothing, her eyes hard. Seamus hesitated a moment before accepting the futility of further argument. Touching the brim of his hat lightly, he left her to her anger.

Mike waited down the deck, his handsome face pinched in concern. As he neared, Seamus spread his hands in a gesture of defeat. "You've got yourself a situation, pal."

The angel nodded. "Gabe thinks you should go back anyway. If you find out how she died, it might convince her this is no trick."

"It might not." Seamus' brows rose, wrinkling his forehead. "I've seen her type before." He grinned weakly. "In fact, I was married to her type."

"Really?" Mike's voice remained casual, but his eyes

sparked with interest.

Like Cassie Parker, Seamus was one of Mike's difficult cases. Unlike Cassie Parker, however, Seamus had no trouble believing he was dead. The problem was with the decision to move on. Those who left the ship became part of something beyond human comprehension. That something required giving up one's individuality, the person each man or woman believed himself to be. As they had in life, the dead had free will. Each person could take as much time as he wanted to think about it.

For reasons he couldn't explain, even to himself, Seamus couldn't give up being Seamus. He remained on the ship, one of many called Portalists, who worked at jobs of their own choosing as they delayed the decision to go on. The elegant lifestyle, the "goodies," to use the popular term, didn't appeal to him. The chance to return to life did.

Seamus ran a finger around his shirt collar and adjusted the knot in his wide, brown tie. The angels might not understand what kept him here, but he served a purpose. And at least *he'd* never refused to believe he was dead.

He returned to the particulars of the present case. "How much do you want to know about Miss Parker?"

Mike considered. "Everything you can get. When she accepts that her life on Earth is over, she'll want to know how she died."

Seamus adjusted his fedora. "I'll get what I can."

"Take your time," Mike advised glumly. "It's going to be a while before this one's ready to listen."

"I'll leave as soon as Gabe gives the okay. While I'm gone" –He put a hand on Mike's shoulder— "have a nice time dealing with a corpse who refuses to cooperate."

With a rueful grin, Mike moved off. Seamus returned to the ship's rail to wait, staring into the beautiful nothing. Colorful mists, almost transparent but not quite, changed constantly in a soft, lazy pattern. They were so delicate it appeared that at any second the colors would resolve, and the watchers would see their destination. The sight was both mesmerizing and calming. He still felt its attraction, even after all this time.

A couple of elderly women passed, possibly on their way to quilting class or Bingo. Others strolled at a leisurely pace, taking in the view as they talked quietly. Along the rail solitary figures leaned, staring outward as they pondered where they'd been and where they were going. Farther down the deck was a lively scene as badminton players shouted encouragement to each other and laughed at near misses.

Pensively silent, busily content. It was a common dichotomy. Despite an infinite variety of things to do on board, most guests spent significant time alone, contemplating unfathomable questions of life and death. Time was a factor in the decision they all had to make. On the ship, details of an individual's life faded unless he made an active effort. After a few days, a person might recall that he liked oatmeal cookies but be unable to remember the grandmother who'd once baked them for him. Forgetting led to acceptance, and as memories of life faded, the choice became easier.

Seamus refused to let that happen to him. Every day, he went over the details of his life carefully, making sure he remembered everything. It took a great deal of effort to hold onto who he'd been and how he'd died, but his determination was strong. To Seamus, life with all its uncertainty and sorrow was better than this perfect existence where a raised voice was a rarity and every day was exactly like the one before.

He'd never shared his reasons for staying with anyone, angel or fellow traveler, remaining apart from others and telling himself he preferred it that way. There were times lately, however, when he wished there was someone to talk to. Twice now he'd returned to life with a partner, and while it hadn't always been easy, he'd liked the company. When Mike sought him out today, Seamus had found himself wishing the angel had someone in mind to go along on the case.

It would be hard to find someone, he thought, setting his foot on the bottom rail. Most Portalists went on when the days of luxury became routine, once they realized the identities they clung to were gone forever. Few stayed as long as Seamus had. Even fewer went back to life, as he did, to serve as detective to the dead.

Seamus knew other cross-backs, but none he'd choose for a partner. Mostly young men eager for adventure, they gathered in groups on deck like members of an exclusive club, chuckling over the private thoughts and secret desires of the living. They weren't bad guys, but Seamus thought it was rude to use the living as hosts and then make fun of them. Unable to defend humanity's silliness but unwilling to defame it, he avoided his fellow cross-backs.

Maybe he could find someone on board who'd be willing to go back and see life one more time. Strolling the deck, Seamus looked at the people around him. Who among them might leave this idyllic place and brave the pain of the crossing to take up the weight of a physical body and the grind of life on earth? There had to be someone. When he finished Cassie Parker's case, he'd see if he could find that person. This time he'd go alone, as he'd done many times before.

That was okay. He was used to it.

Chapter Two

CROSSING BACK WAS BAD, but if a guy knew the pain was coming and rolled with it, he could tolerate it. Still, getting stretched into smoke, or something even wispier than smoke, was no fun, even though he'd done it lots of times.

When the pain faded and he opened his eyes, Seamus found himself among a jumble of items that made no sense. It was dark, a single blue light overhead the only illumination. Beside him was a wall that seemed real at first, but then he saw it was only about eight feet square with wheels on the bottom. Behind him, an antique couch sat on one end of a rectangular rug. A nearby table held various small items: a handkerchief with lace edges, a couple of delicate fans, an oil lamp with a plush velvet shade, and a long-stemmed clay pipe. Mechanical devices and pulleys, hulking shapes in the dimness, took up much of the space behind him.

He was backstage at a theatre, the place where Cassie

Parker's life had ended and his work would begin. He listened for movement. Since a cross-back no longer existed on Earth, he had to find a host within a few seconds or return to the ship. Knowing how the system operated, Seamus trusted someone would be there.

A bump and a muttered exclamation told him someone was. Propelling himself toward the sound, he melded with his first host of the trip. As Seamus' presence hit, she put one hand on her stomach and the other on her forehead. "Lord," she said aloud.

Not even close, Seamus answered silently. He felt the shift from being weightless to being human: slow movements, the pressure of gravity, and the drag of thoughts that must be processed, looped through past experiences and operative synapses, and formed into words by the slow workings of mortal thought. Coming back to earth was like being tossed into a vat of Brylcreem.

It took only a few seconds to determine that his host was the building's cleaning woman. In her hands were the tools of her trade: a bucket of cleaning supplies, a dust mop, and a broom. Setting them down center stage with a careless clatter, she adjusted to his presence with the determination of one long used to working no matter how shaky she felt. Fumbling through the sets to an interior wall, she found a switch, snapped it to one side, and the area filled with light.

Moving around the fake wall, the woman approached a heavy curtain. A large *X* formed with fluorescent tape marked its center, presumably to let those behind it know where it parted. The woman surveyed the stage, judging the amount of work to be done. Opening the curtains a slit, she looked out at the empty, silent auditorium, estimating the time she'd need to spend out there. The lighted exit signs faintly illuminated the seating area, which Seamus guessed could accommodate as many as two hundred fifty people with about fifty more seats in the balcony. It was a small theatre, but where?

While the woman, whose name was Fay Winters, cleaned the stage, Seamus tuned in to her thoughts, or tried to. Although a cross-back couldn't actually read a host's mind, Seamus usually got passing bits of thought that led to a capsulized version of current events, especially when there'd been a recent death. From this host he got so little that he wondered briefly if she suspected his presence and was blocking him.

No. Mrs. Winters simply didn't think about much but dust, used chewing gum, paint splotches, and wood polish, either with or without scratch cover.

She opened the front curtain, banishing the closed-in feel of the stage, and spritzed the floor with a concoction meant to trap dust in cotton fibers. Pushing the wide mop in front of her left, then right, then left again, she cleared the wooden surface of dust, some feathers, and a few fallen rhinestones. When it was done, she examined her handiwork and nodded, satisfied. Then, to Seamus' surprise, she did a song-and-dance chorus of "One" for an audience of none, leaving out the words she didn't know.

"One, similar sensation, every simple move she takes..." The performance pleased her as much as it horrified Seamus. Had no one ever told the woman she couldn't carry a tune even with a bucket in one hand?

Done warbling, Mrs. Winters finally had a thought that interested him. Should she clean the auditorium next or the lobby? On that Seamus had an opinion, and he whispered softly, "Lobby." Though he couldn't force a host to do as he wanted, a suggestion at the right moment could be effective if he kept it subtle. Anything more might convince his host she was losing her mind.

He was pleased when Mrs. Winters muttered aloud, "I'll do the front next."

The lobby was small and slightly tawdry. The building had once been a factory of some kind, with brick walls, stamped-metal ceilings, and the remains of ancient mechanical supports overhead. Seamus caught the smell of old machine oil in the corners.

No attempt had been made to make it pretty, which he guessed meant it was supposed to be trendy. There was a wainscoted ticket booth; a curved bar that offered boxed candies, bagged snacks, and cans of soda; a tiny cloakroom; and glamorous, heavily retouched portraits on most of the available wall space. Above the ticket booth in flowing, hard-to-read script, were the words, "The Vic: Toronto's Victorian Theatre." That explained the fainting couch.

So he was in Canada. Had Cassie Parker sounded Canadian? Seamus had lived most of his life in Chicago, so he could usually detect the accent, but she hadn't said enough to him to give much of a sample.

A sharp knock sounded at the front door, and Mrs. Winters lumbered over and peered out through the glass.

"Inspector Terry Nordman." The man on the other side showed his police identification. When the cleaning lady opened the door, Seamus immediately jumped to the inspector, having learned enough about pine-scented versus orange-scented cleaners to last an eternity.

He settled in with Nordman, making himself small while the man gulped down the nausea an extra presence caused him. After only a few seconds, the inspector resumed his business-like demeanor. "You know a young woman died here yesterday."

"Yeah. The manager called to say I shouldn't clean in the back till you finish." She turned and led the way into the auditorium and toward the stage.

As they walked, Nordman asked, "Did you know Ms. Parker?"

Mrs. Winters shrugged. "Talked to her a few times. She was nice, not like some."

"Did everyone like her, then?"

"Oh, sure." She grinned. "She's the one made everybody look good."

"She did the costumes."

"A regular wizard! I used to sew for my kids, but nothing

like her. She could make a piece of burlap look like something."

"Huh." The inspector seemed uninterested in the finer points of costume design.

"Neen says she hit her head back there." Mrs. Winters pointed toward the stage.

"Apparently she was finding her way in the dark and ran into a set piece that was out of place," Nordman said.

"What would that be?"

Nordman gestured toward the east wall. "The guillotine."

Mrs. Winters shivered. "I hated that thing from the first! I said to Dick—that's my husband—I said, 'Why did they build something so awful?'"

"I was told it's necessary for the final scene of *A Tale of Two Cities*."

"It's gruesome," she said, brows low and lips tight in disapproval. "Gives me the creeps every time I pass by it, hanging up there like doom!"

She led the way to the stage, climbing the five steps at the right side. Seamus felt pain jolt through Nordman's right knee as he lifted his weight up each riser. There was joint replacement in the man's future.

Mrs. Winters disappeared into a corner for a moment, and the backstage lights came on. "Hard to find the switches back there," she remarked. "Easy to get hurt wandering around in the dark." Obviously not the type to dwell on such things, she approached the heavy black cyclorama, a C-shaped curtain that shielded the backstage from audience view. She pushed it around to the opposite wall, exposing the whole stage area. "There, that's the best we can do for light."

The part of the stage the public never saw was divided into sections, each containing the set for a scene in the current play. Seamus pictured a well-rehearsed crew changing scenes in almost complete darkness, moving it into place with only muted thumps and the occasional squeak of friction on ropes or wheels.

Fastened high on the right-hand wall was a large framework he hadn't noticed earlier. Almost full size, the guillotine hung crookedly against the battered brick wall. A projecting pipe left from the building's factory days was its anchor point, and two lengths of plastic-coated metal chain held it in place.

Nordman approached the set piece. Wires attached to

the top of its wooden frame and led to a pulley above center stage. When released from its fastenings on the wall, the guillotine would swing out over the stage like a pendulum. A black rope attached to its base acted as a guide, so stagehands could stop the heavy piece when it reached the center of the stage and lower it to the floor.

"I came to see how this thing works now that everyone's out of the way." Nordman peered into the shadows above the stage. "Why didn't they hang it directly overhead, so they could just raise it and lower it when they need to?"

Mrs. Winters pointed to a large flyer above them painted with a flowery outdoor scene. "They have to pull it aside, or it gets in the way of Lucy's garden coming down."

"I see."

For the next few minutes, Nordman experimented with the guillotine, unhooking the chains that secured it, lifting it from the pipe, and letting it swing to center stage with different levels of force applied on the control rope. The last time, with a warning to Mrs. Winters, he let it swing without any counterweight. Unhindered, it made a wide arc across the stage. It was obvious the heavy piece might well injure someone crossing its path. *Or kill her*, Seamus thought.

That solved the "how" of Cassie's death. She'd never have known what hit her.

As Nordman worked, Seamus gleaned from his thoughts facts that helped him understand the situation. Sometime in the morning, Cassie Parker had come backstage, presumably to assure that costume items were in place for the next show. As she made her way toward the light switch, the guillotine, improperly secured on its overhead hook, had come loose and swung down, striking her on the head and killing her.

"How would Miss Parker have gotten in?" Nordman asked Mrs. Winters.

"After some break-ins a few years ago, they put burglar bars on the main entrances." She led Nordman to the back corner of the building. "They replaced the old wooden door back here with this reinforced metal one. Here's where she'd have come in."

He opened the door to peer out at the alley and then pulled it closed with a metallic shudder. "This is the employee entrance?"

The woman nodded. "Cassie had a key, 'cause she worked all kind of crazy hours."

"Who else has one?"

She raised fingers as she counted. "Neen, Albert, the sound guy, the light tech, me."

Nordman traced the route the woman would have taken. "Maybe her slamming the door caused enough vibration to shake the guillotine loose."

He spoke to himself, but Mrs. Winters shook her frizzy curls in agreement. "Yeah, 'specially if it wasn't fastened right after they used it last."

Nordman nodded, accepting the most logical scenario. It had been the woman's bad luck to walk directly into the path of the piece she'd jolted free. A sad accident. Nordman had a moment of pity for Cassie. He hoped she'd died immediately, and wondered if she might have been saved if someone had been in the building with her. *Alone is a bad way to die*, he thought.

But it's the way we all do it, Seamus added. *There's really no way to die together.*

Seamus wasn't as certain as the inspector was that Cassie's death had been accidental. He wondered what the odds were that in an almost-empty theatre, the guillotine set piece would come loose at the exact moment someone moved into its path. Seamus wanted to know who had secured that set piece, and if that person had any sort of grudge against Cassie Parker.

Mrs. Winters' mind had moved on to the living and her workload. "Are you going to let them do the evening show?"

"I spoke with the cast and crew last night," Nordman replied. Seamus picked up on his memories of those interviews. Many had been upset to the point of tears, a couple near hysteria. No one mentioned any bad feelings between Cassie and anyone else. All agreed she'd done her job well. Again Nordman thought, *A terrible accident.*

The forensic people had done their tests. The guillotine's front right leg had blood and hair where it connected with Cassie's head. If it had indeed come loose from its fasteners at the moment she walked into its path, it would have swung at the perfect level to cause the wound on her skull.

"I don't see why we should keep these people from making a living."

"That's what I told Dick," Mrs. Winters said. "People can't do their jobs when the place is shut down. It was bad, but—" Seamus sensed the platitude coming "—the show must go on."

A soft sound came from the auditorium, and someone said, "Excuse me?"

Nordman turned to see a young woman standing in the center aisle wearing a red, parka-like coat and shoes not suited for trudging through snow. A suitcase sat beside her, the handle extended for pulling. Having met the decedent, Seamus knew immediately the woman must be Cassie Parker's sister, probably her twin.

"Yes?" Nordman said, his voice filling the room in a testament to good acoustics.

"I'm Christy Parker. I'm here about my sister." With that, she began to cry.

Chapter Three

Seamus settled into the mind of Christy Parker, who apologized for her tears even as they fell.

"That's all right, Miss Parker," Nordman assured. "It's a terrible shock."

"Yes." She dug a fresh tissue from a small black clutch purse and wiped her eyes. "I stayed with friends in Burlington last night. I was supposed to meet Cass here today."

"We tried to reach you at your home, but you must have already been on the way."

"I have a cell phone now, but apparently she forgot to add it to her contact sheet."

"I'll need that number."

"Here." She dug in the purse again, found a card, and handed it over.

As Christy pulled herself together, Nordman scanned the card and put it into his breast pocket. "There's a little café across the street where we can talk if you like. I'll try to answer your questions."

"Thank you." Christy turned the suitcase around.

"She can leave that here." Mrs. Winters spoke to Nordman, as if Christy were deaf. Seamus guessed she was embarrassed to speak to the recently bereaved. "I'll put it in the office, and she can pick it up anytime."

"I appreciate it." Christy handed the cleaning lady her case. Nordman followed her up the aisle, and they left the dark theatre for the bright December sunshine.

Once they were settled in the café, Nordman told Christy, "This is what we call a reportable death, Miss. Any fatal accident in the workplace must be investigated. The OFPS, Ontario pathology, has your sister's body, and they'll be reporting their findings as soon as possible." Nordman went on, explaining Cassie's death frankly but not in great detail. Although Seamus hadn't spent much time with the inspector, he thought they shared the belief that with violent death, the less loved ones knew, the better.

"Human beings do it every day." Nordman took a sip of his cinnamon-flavored coffee while Christy pretty much ignored her Jamaican blend. "We drive with our attention diverted, take the stairs too fast, run outside in slippers to get the paper on an icy winter day." He met her gaze directly. "Who'd guess a person could lose her life doing such a simple thing?"

Seamus could find no guilt in Christy Parker, nor did she seem aware of anything in her sister's life that might suggest her death was anything but an accident. She was distracted, and he sensed she'd dealt with a lot lately. She was in shock over her sister's death. There was something sad that had to do with her father too. In addition to that, the city itself gave her the jitters. Deciding Nordman was more likely to lead him to facts about Cassie's death, Seamus jumped back to him.

Through the inspector's eyes, Seamus watched Cassie Parker's twin shake her head slightly as his departure lightened her mind somewhat. "I planned to stay with Cassie for a couple of weeks, but now I don't know what to do," she told Nordman. "Our father died—just over a week ago. Home doesn't feel like home right now." She waved a hand as if to banish more tears.

"Can you go back to your friends' place?"

She looked doubtful. "I'm sure they'll ask me to, but

they've got kids and dogs and jobs. They don't need a grieving house guest."

Nordman nodded understanding. "There's your sister's place. We're finished with it."

"You searched Cassie's apartment?"

"Just to be thorough." Nordman made a calming gesture with his hands. "We found nothing unusual. The landlord tells me the rent is paid for several months, and it might be a few days before your sister's body is released. You could stay there, as you planned."

"No, Inspector," Christy said, her voice becoming thick with tears. "Not as I planned, but thank you for the suggestion. I might do that."

CASSIE DEBATED keeping her second appointment with Nancy. It was so stupid, sitting down in the lovely office full of completely real and touchable furniture and talking about being dead. She could not for the life of her (an odd phrase, under the circumstances) comprehend how these people thought they'd convince her she was in some other-worldly limbo. She knew reality when she saw it, and being employed at a theatre, she knew a little about setting a scene too.

After the first meeting with Nancy, she'd begun looking for a way to escape. There were apparently no restrictions on what she could do and where she could go, but she could find no way off the ship. It had no lifeboats, which she was pretty sure was against the law. She'd been unable to locate a radio room or any other means of communicating with the mainland. The only escape was overboard, and although she could swim, she had no idea where land was.

When it was time for her second appointment with her counselor, Cassie ran a hairbrush over her short hair, unwilling to appear in public in a state of disarray, no matter the situation. The brush was almost like the one she had at home, with firm bristles and a round handle. It must be costing these people a fortune to rent a ship, staff it with actors, and create the special-effects-whatever that surrounded the ship like a hypnotic cloud. She'd seen movies where elaborate ruses were perpetrated on poor slobs to convince them to drop their guard and tell what they knew, but she had no secrets, no connection to high-level espionage, and no friends in high government positions. In fact, she was down a few friends just lately, although only one of them had mattered.

So why should she go and talk to this Nancy, who claimed to be a guidance angel?

"Because I'm curious," she said aloud. "And besides, what else do I have to do?"

Cassie knocked on Nancy's office door exactly on time, at 9:00 a.m. Hearing the calm voice call out, "Come in," she entered, approached the desk, and sat in the same velvety chair she'd fidgeted in yesterday while Nancy explained that she was dead and had entered "the process," a link between life and eternity. She would, Nancy said, remain on the ship until she was ready to "go on" to something unimaginably better. None of it made the tiniest bit of sense, especially since Cassie knew for a fact she wasn't dead. She'd felt her face flush as Nancy told those lies. Dead people don't feel warm. Angry people do.

She'd returned hoping for answers, but Cassie doubted she'd get anything close to the truth.

Everything in Nancy's office looked the same as it had yesterday, except Nancy's outfit was peach-colored rather than pale yellow. A dozen lilies in a vase by the door added a faint, pleasant scent to the room. "Hello, Cassie," Nancy greeted her. "Did you get some rest?"

"A little." She didn't admit she'd paced her cabin most of the night, fearing sleep lest they sneak in with syringes and inject her with truth serum. The whole thing was insane. Neen and Donna would be wondering where she was, and her sister had arrived in Toronto by now and was probably frantic to find Cassie missing. Christy would be lost without her twin to guide her.

"Sleep is beneficial," Nancy was saying. "You don't really need it here, since the form you're given is only an approximation of what you had on earth, but we find that people are comforted by doing things they're used to doing. Hence the ship and the amenities provided."

Cassie had observed people on board doing all sorts of restful things: swimming, bowling, even learning to dance. She'd remained apart from everyone. Obviously, no one here could be trusted.

Since waking yesterday morning, she'd spoken to only three people: Rudy, the steward who apprised her of her appointment with Nancy and explained the ship's amenities; a strangely-dressed guy who'd approached her at the ship's rail and tried to start a conversation; and Nancy herself. When she'd tried to question Rudy, he'd referred her to Nancy, insisting it wasn't his place to explain things. She wondered briefly if the guy in the old-time suit might have given her a hint or two. He'd seemed the type who'd find out what was going on no matter who told him not to. Too bad she'd been in a rotten mood and sent him away.

It would have to be Nancy who answered her questions. She certainly looked competent, sort of like Helen Mirren, an actress Cassie had always admired. When she'd become agitated at the end of their first interview, Nancy had remained calm, merely suggesting she take time to think things over. Now, Nancy studied Cassie's face, apparently judging her mood.

"What have you been doing since yesterday?" Nancy asked.

Cassie examined her hands. "I walked around the ship, looked at everything."

"I hope you had some breakfast. They tell me the buffet's very good."

She'd smelled it as she passed along the corridor: eggs, bacon, and cinnamon, among other tempting odors. "I didn't feel much like eating."

"And yesterday? Did you eat anything at all?"

"No. That guy Rudy invited me to go to the dining room, but I didn't want to. I let him bring me a salad." She didn't add that she hadn't touched it. Oddly, a day and a half since her last meal, she wasn't hungry at all. What was the reason for that? She couldn't really be—

Cassie squared her shoulders. No. She was alive and fully capable of eating. She just didn't want to with all that was going on.

"What questions do you have for me?" Nancy's hands lay on the desktop, still, pale, and without spots or wrinkles, despite the fact that she had to be over sixty.

"I don't understand all this." A surge of rebellion made her add with an angry wave of her hand, "And I know I'm not dead, so don't start that again."

Nancy must have seen that simply repeating yesterday's revelations wouldn't help. "Why don't you tell me the last thing you remember? Maybe that will help us understand what happened."

"There isn't anything. I went to the theatre to work, and then I woke up here." Again Cassie reminded herself not to tell these people anything important. If they were trying to trick her into telling—*What?* She asked herself. *The Vic isn't exactly Interpol Headquarters.*

"Tell me what you remember."

Blowing out a long breath, Cassie clasped her hands under her chin. "I came in early because one of the women in the cast lost part of her costume. She's always losing stuff and throwing a fit about it, and after the evening show she was going off like a madwoman. I told her to go home. I figured I'd come in early and find it before she got there and started whining, you know?"

It occurred to her that if she were really an angel, Nancy wouldn't know. But Nancy was *not* an angel. Cassie went on, "Our backstage lights are at the front of the stage, so if you come in the back way, you kind of have to feel your way through to the front to turn them on. Heading toward them is the last thing I remember." She almost said, "That's when you guys kidnapped me," but Nancy didn't strike her as a kidnapper. Then again, didn't bad guys try to act nice so they could find out what they wanted to know? She fought the urge to rub her throbbing temples, unwilling to appear nervous. What were these people after?

"I am not dead," she said aloud. "I feel fine."

"As I explained yesterday, Cassie, you are dead. You feel fine because we have provided you with a representation of your former self." Nancy's voice was calm, her face serious.

"I feel fine." She repeated it through clenched teeth. "Normal. Alive."

Nancy nodded. "For people like you, those who die in the prime of life, it's difficult. If you were older, if you'd had a bad back or macular degeneration, you'd be able to perceive the improvement."

"What do you mean?"

"There is no physical illness here, no pain."

"I am *not* dead. And wherever here is, it isn't heaven." Cassie tried to think what she could say or do to convince this so-called angel that her tricks would not succeed. She might have thrown something, but there was nothing to throw. Perhaps they'd faced that problem before.

Realizing she'd been wrong to come here, Cassie rose. "There's nothing you can do to convince me I'm dead." She leaned toward Nancy, resting her hands on the smooth desktop. "So just stop it."

Nancy tilted her head to the side like a robot that didn't

comprehend a command. As Cassie started for the door she said, "I could recommend people you might speak with."

Cassie stopped with her hand on the doorknob. "People you've coached to say all the right things? Don't even try it."

Nancy looked up at her calmly. "We would never force you to interact with anyone."

"Good. That's good," Cassie spoke distinctly. "I want you to leave me alone: you and Rudy and whoever else you've got lined up."

Nancy's expression changed at her mention of Rudy. "I hope your steward hasn't been pushy. They're asked to focus on the amenities, not on metaphysical aspects of the crossing."

Cassie put up a hand. "No, Rudy's fine, really. I just—" She clamped the hand on her head as if the top might blow off. "I need some time to myself."

"Of course you do." Nancy seemed sincere. "I won't schedule you again, but feel free to return any time. I'm always available."

The only thing Cassie wanted to say in response was too childish to be uttered aloud: "Don't hold your breath, Angel."

Chapter Four

WHEN SHE LEFT THE CAFÉ where she'd talked with the police inspector, Christy looked around for a subway station marker. She'd been to Toronto a few times before, but always with Cassie. Now she wished she'd paid more attention to the routes they'd taken. The apartment was on Bloor, only a few stops from the theatre, so that should be easy. As costume mistress, Cassie had spent many hours in the old building, drawing, planning, cutting, and sewing. Because of that, she lived as close as possible to the Vic.

One of the most enjoyable parts of Christy's visits had been going with her twin to second-hand stores, one after another, searching out bits and pieces for costumes. She'd been proud of some of her finds: dresses that suited particular characters; a frock coat, improbably found hanging among leisure suits and tweed jackets in the men's section; and a treasure trove of old costume jewelry. It had been worth a few sneezes from dusty old fabrics to hear Cass squeal with joy at her successes.

"We don't have much of a budget," Cassie had confided. "Whenever we find something that works, it saves me time and the company money."

When costumes couldn't be scavenged or rented, it was Cassie's job to make the outfit that fit the role, the play, and the scene perfectly. Her costumes were always a hit, from Fagin's natty-tatty suit to Lady Windermere's exquisite gowns.

Cass had discovered her fashion talents as a kid in 4-H, when a woman from a farm outside Fairfield offered sewing classes. Though both girls had taken to it, Cassie announced when high school ended that making costumes would be her career. By that time, their father had developed COPD from years of smoking. Christy had stayed with him, taking a job at the local grocery store and sporadic classes at a nearby college. She'd told herself she wasn't the type to live in a big city like Toronto.

"Excuse me." A voice at her back caused her to turn. "Aren't you Christy?"

It took a few seconds to return to the present and the man before her. Harold? Harlan?

"I'm Henry Spellman, remember?" He gestured at the theatre. "I worked with Cassie."

Henry Spellman had shown up for her father's funeral, held only a week ago. It had been a shock to learn that he and her twin were in a relationship, because Cass hadn't mentioned it. Christy figured her sister felt guilty about the turns their lives had taken. Cass had had a job she loved, a life that was moving forward, and a man who loved her. Christy had none of those things.

She tried to recall what she'd learned on the day of the funeral. Henry was the male lead in the company, and he was currently playing Charles Darnay in *A Tale of Two Cities*. She'd thought it was nice of him to drive up for the funeral, but Cassie had acted embarrassed, like she wished he hadn't come. Christy understood her feelings. It should have been just the two of them saying goodbye to Dad. Still, it had been nice of Henry to make the effort.

Spellman looked exactly like the honorable, lovable Charles Darnay should: wide shoulders, noble chin, high brow, lightly waving blondish hair, and a direct, honest gaze. He wasn't smiling now, but she remembered his smile was warm and candid. After giving her a moment to place him, Henry said, "I'm really, really sorry about Cassie."

"Thank you." Her eyes filled with tears, but she controlled herself with determined effort. People from Fairfield, Ontario, staunch farmers of strong stock, did not melt down on the public sidewalk.

She heard Henry's shoes scuff against the snow-melt crystals on the pavement. "I was wondering if I could come by later. I mean, if you're staying at Cassie's place."

Christy hesitated. She wasn't ready to talk with Cassie's boyfriend, to learn the secrets her sister had kept from her. "I'm sorry," she said. "I'm going to be busy for a while."

He was disappointed, but he didn't press. "I understand. If you ever need anything—" Reaching into an inside pocket, Spellman pulled out a card and handed it to her. "Here's my number. I mean it. Anything." He backed up a few steps, blue eyes holding hers briefly, then turned and walked away.

Christy put the card into her purse and closed it with a firm click. Remembering her sister's frequent lectures about safety in the city, she set the purse under her arm.

The thought that Cassie was dead returned like a hammer blow. How could it have happened? Her beloved, only sister killed in a freak accident that should have resulted in a bump and a funny story. Coming so soon after their father's death, it was crushing. How unfair could life be?

Maybe she should just go home to Fairfield. A few hours' ride to the northwest, her home town charmed tourists with its stone-built houses and the lovely river that divided it neatly in two. People there would cluck over her losses and welcome her back into their familiar routines. Was that what she wanted?

Toronto, on the other hand, was big and a little frightening. Cassie had loved it and always said that Fairfield was a nice place to grow up, but she'd be gone from there as soon as possible. Cass would never have blamed the city for what happened to her. Christy could almost hear her voice in her ear, "I could just as easily have died from a bump on the head in Fairfield. That's life, Chris. It ends when it ends."

After their mother died of a massive stroke when they were fifteen, Cassie had for a time become fascinated with the subject of death. She'd read a variety of books about it, everything from the *Bible* to Mary Roach's *Spook*, trying to decide what she believed about the afterlife. She'd always added with raised brows, "If there is one."

Her quest for understanding had been a trial for both Christy and Earl, their father. She'd frequently quizzed them about their beliefs, throwing out bits of information from various sources. Finally, Earl had refused to discuss the subject further. "We'll find out, in our time," he insisted. When Cass mumbled something about it being too long to wait, he'd said with a chuckle, "Less for me than for you, God willing." Christy recalled her teenage self, horrified at Dad's ability to joke about his own death.

Now they were both gone, with hardly any distance at all between their "times." Christy, who pretty much accepted what everyone else believed--some sort of life after death and some sort of judging process accompanying it--now wondered exactly where her sister's essence was. Surely, such a strong personality as Cass Parker did not just dissipate into the air.

A noisy truck jarred Christy from her reverie, and she looked up. Henry Spellman had stopped at the theatre entrance and was looking back at her with a curious expression. Remembering she'd said she had things to do,

Christy turned and headed toward the subway.

NORDMAN RETURNED TO THE STATION, which hummed with the activity of police agencies everywhere, a quiet busy-ness that Seamus found comforting. He made some calls to update his notes on Cassie Parker's death, learning that the guillotine had indeed struck the fatal blow, and there was no other evidence of violence. "A few inches one way or the other, she might have lived through it," he was told. *Won't tell the sister that,* Seamus heard in the inspector's thoughts. *Too sad.*

Next he reviewed the interview notes from the previous day. Putting together what he saw, Seamus learned that Cassie had a boyfriend until recently, when he'd thrown her over for one of the actresses. It was a rotten thing to do, several had opined, since she'd been away tending her dying father. Still, Cassie hadn't been particularly broken-hearted, according to a woman named Donna who'd repeated Cassie's comment on the day before she died: "It was just a thing, and now it's over."

Nordman was beginning to think in terms of closing the

case. There was nothing to suggest Cassie Parker had been murdered. Though he didn't know why, Seamus wasn't yet convinced. It would have been nice if he could actually talk to Nordman, lay their ideas out together and discuss them, but that was impossible. Hosts were likely to conclude they were crazy if they heard voices inside their head. Still, he missed the exchange of information he used to have with other cops, the what-ifs and why-nots of criminal investigation.

The phone rang. "Nordman."

"Hey, it's Duane. We caught a break on the Torson thing."

"Really?" A note of excitement entered Nordman's voice.

"Police out in Cambridge found a body. Want to come look?"

Nordman closed the computer file he'd started on Cassie Parker. "I'll be right there."

As the inspector gathered his things, Seamus realized he'd made a mistake. Though he was conscientious enough, the inspector wasn't focused on Cassie Parker. Almost certain her death had been an accident, he was merely going through the motions. Now, with a break in a case he'd been working on for months, he forgot her entirely. As Nordman rose to leave, wincing slightly at the pain that stabbed through his bum knee, Seamus wished he'd stayed at the theatre, where Cassie's death was sure to be a frequent topic of conversation.

For the rest of the day, Seamus chafed at being imprisoned in the wrong head. He considered trying to make his way to the Vic by jumping randomly from person to person, but that was tricky. He could end up farther from his goal rather than closer. Despite his disinterest in Cassie Parker's death, Nordman was his best chance to reach either the theatre or the sister. He'd simply have to wait.

CASSIE LEFT NANCY'S OFFICE at a pace much faster than necessary. She was angry at them all, and if she admitted it to herself, a little afraid too. What did these people want with her? Why had they invented this crazy scenario and gone to so much trouble?

She headed for the elevator that would take her back to her stateroom, which seemed like a haven right now. She could lock the door and remove herself from the others on the ship, although she should probably assume there was surveillance everywhere. *What* did they *want*?

The impact was so sudden she grunted in surprise. Heedless of her speed and the path ahead, she'd collided with someone at the intersection of two corridors. When she'd collected herself, Cassie saw an older woman sprawled on the floor, a surprised expression on her face.

"I'm so sorry!" Cassie bent to help her up. "Are you hurt?"

The woman rose with agility that belied her obvious age. "No, no. I'm perfectly fine." She smiled. "No pain here, you know, but the laws of physics still apply."

Good grief. The whole heaven thing again, Cassie thought. She bent to retrieve the woman's tapestry bag and the things that had spilled out of it. Mostly it was books. Handing over a copy of *The Dancing Wu Li Masters*, she said, "I've heard of that one. Pretty deep, right?"

"But good." The woman put it back into the bag. "I was returning them to the library."

Cassie picked up the rest, six books in all. "I take it you like to read?"

She grinned. "When you get to a certain point in life, there isn't much else to like!" Her drawl betrayed a

Southern background, and her brown skin was finely wrinkled and generously freckled from a lifetime in the sun.

Cassie handed her the last two books, Dickens' *Great Expectations* and Mike Wallace's *Between You and Me: a Memoir*. "Quite an eclectic selection there."

"Got all the time I want to read now." She put out a hand. "I'm Ruth Waycliff."

Cassie took Ruth's hand, so thin it felt unreal. "Cassie Parker."

"From—?"

"Toronto."

"A Yankee." The term was accompanied by a smile to remove any possible sting.

Responding to her warm manner, Cassie smiled for the first time since arriving. "Do Canadians count as Yankees?"

"I'm a Texan. You're all Yankees to me." She glanced over Cassie's shoulder. "You new here?"

"Since yesterday morning." She was wondering if Ruth was a victim, like she was.

"You came from Nancy's office just now?"

Cassie looked at her in surprise. "You know about Nancy?"

"Sure. We all meet with her at the beginning."

"And do you believe the cr—the stuff she's peddling?"

Ruth examined Cassie's face for a few moments. "Believe I'm dead? I sure do, darlin'! Dying was the best thing to happen to me in the last fifteen years!"

CHRISTY FOUND AND BOARDED the correct subway train with no trouble. She even knew enough to buy a pass from the machine in the lobby so she could ride for several days without buying a token each time. She knew the stop nearest her sister's place and was only a little nervous about getting there without Cassie's confident presence. The quiet hiss as the doors closed and the hum as the train took off reassured her, and she told herself, *You can do this.*

The people on the car were the usual mix of business types, shoppers, and students. No one paid anyone else any attention at all, at least at first. But after Christy sat down on an unoccupied bench seat of molded plastic, a man who'd apparently been sleeping at the opposite end of the car opened an eye, watched her for a few seconds, then came across the car to sit next to her. He said nothing, but his body intruded into her space, thigh touching hers, shoulder pressing shoulder. Christy pulled herself toward the wall, shifting her purse to the opposite side. When the train made its first stop, the man moved even closer, causing her to lean into the wall and turn her shoulder toward the window. She didn't want to appear rude, but still.

When the train started up, the man shifted even closer, so near she could smell the booze on his breath. He didn't speak, but his grin, and the path of his gaze, slowly from her eyes to her body and back up, spoke volumes about his character.

Christy considered her options. In order to move, she'd have to push past him, and she guessed he'd make that as unpleasant as possible.

She could call for help, but what would she say? That the guy was looking at her? She'd feel like an idiot.

Cassie would have put him in his place with a few well-chosen words, but Christy wasn't Cass. She had no stomach for confrontation. She would just have to ignore him.

Then she felt pressure on her thigh. Glancing sideways, she saw that her tormentor appeared to be focused on the map of the transit system over the door. Still, she could feel his warm, damp hand against her leg, even through her jeans. She cringed but was unable to move any farther away. Pressing herself against the wall of the car, she wondered, should she make a fuss? Again she decided it was best to ignore the man. Her stop was next after this one.

The train slowed, hissed to a halt, and the doors opened. The man's hand pressed harder, as if the force of the slowing car was responsible. Then they were off again. *Just a little farther*, Christy told herself.

The hand moved slightly upward, toward the top of her thigh, and she bit back a sob. This was not accidental, no matter what she'd tried to tell herself. The train swayed, and the hand moved up a little more. She had to do something.

Putting one hand to her stomach, Christy turned toward him and said softly, "You might want to give me some room. I can never predict when the nausea's going to hit."

The stubbly face went from a leer to a frown. "Huh?"

"The doctor says it will go away in the second trimester, but right now—" She raised the hand from her stomach to her mouth, pressing it against her lips. Her body spasmed, and her eyes went wide.

Rising like he had a spring in his backside, the man retreated to his original place. Slapping his skinny butt into the seat, he looked back at Christy, who now stared at the subway map as if it was the most fascinating thing ever. As he chewed on an already ragged fingernail, he glared at her, unsure whether he'd been tricked or not.

The announcement for her stop came over the speaker, and Christy rose with a few others, moving to the doorway in order to make a quick exit. People waiting to get on the train gave them leeway before boarding, and soon Toronto's efficient transportation system rolled on, leaving her on the platform as her recent adversary glared through the window. Checking the signs, Christy climbed the stairs to the correct street exit. From there she could see Cassie's building.

As she approached the apartment, Christy realized she'd left her suitcase at the theatre. Fingering the key Cassie'd given her, she decided it didn't matter. Almost everything her twin owned would work for her, whether clothing or toiletries. Tomorrow, she'd be better able to face Cassie's friends and coworkers at the Vic.

The smell of lemon oil stopped her cold when she

unlocked the door. *She cleaned because I was coming.* It struck her like a blow to the chest. Closing herself inside Cassie's apartment, Christy collapsed on the tweedy sofa in tears.

Chapter Five

BACK IN HER STATEROOM, Cassie thought she might go crazy. Nancy told the wildest sort of lies, and she was getting away with it. The woman she'd met, Ruth, seemed like a nice person, but she actually thought she was dead. They'd convinced the poor old thing with their sets and their serious faces.

As waves of anger washed over her, she succumbed to the urge to throw things. There was little in the room that gave satisfaction, but she threw the bottles of toiletries, the pillows, the TV remote, and even the hair dryer at the wall opposite her bed. None of it did much damage. Storming back and forth, she kicked the things that lay scattered around the room.

"I am NOT dead," she said aloud. "I am getting out of here somehow. I'm going HOME!" As she said the last words, an alternative meaning registered. "Going home" was a euphemism for dying. Sitting down on the bed, she remained motionless for some time, trying to puzzle it out.

A while later, her reverie was interrupted by Rudy, who apologized for bothering her but wanted to offer a list of activities she might like. She refused, probably more curtly than he deserved. The steward was probably a low-level goon, not smart enough to be trusted with the secrets of whoever recruited him and perpetrated this scam. There was no sense quizzing him, but after he left, she was sorry she'd treated him badly. He seemed really disappointed that she wouldn't sample the wonders of the cruise.

She did, however, become sick of the four walls after a couple of hours. Thinking wasn't making things any clearer, but maybe a walk would. She'd gone out on the deck a couple of times now. The air out there smelled nice, though she couldn't identify what the fragrance was. It made her think they were offshore at some exotic port, maybe Tripoli or Bahrain. Was that it? Did these people plan to sell them as slaves to some Third World country?

That didn't make sense. Most of the people she'd seen so far were old. Not good slave material.

It was peaceful on deck, and despite the dire possibilities of her situation, she found it relaxing. There were people around, but no one did more than nod and smile as they passed. Except for the guy who looked like an escapee from a Jimmy Cagney movie, no one had approached her out here. Maybe Nancy had warned them about her.

She wandered without purpose for perhaps twenty minutes, watching people without making eye contact. Some played games, shouting and laughing at hits or misses. Others sat in low chairs, talking or reading. No one was in a hurry. No one seemed agitated or worried. Didn't they know they were prisoners of a band of lunatics or criminals or criminal lunatics?

Cassie missed her sister. She longed for someone she could trust, someone to talk to about all this. These people were like sheep, accepting what they were told and going off to play shuffleboard. Chris was a little naïve sometimes, but she was nobody's fool. Together, they would have figured this out.

As Cassie's gaze swept the faces, looking for any sign that they understood the weirdness of the situation, she saw a familiar mop of gray hair in a circle of laughing people. "Ruth?"

Ruth turned toward her and then smiled in recognition.

"Cassie, isn't it?"

The words tumbled out before she could stop them. "I wonder if we could talk."

Ruth rose and excused herself from the group. "Let's go get something to drink. I'm dying of thirst." She elbowed Cassie lightly as the last sentence registered. "Guess I'm gonna have to change a few figures of speech."

Ruth started off into the ship's interior, her pace sprightly for one so old. As they went down a long corridor, she pointed to a set of double doors. "That's the gym and spa. We're welcome to swim or workout anytime." Later she pointed to the right, at a door marked *Precious Memories*. It was edged with scenic photographs. "That's a neat place. If you miss something, like trees or mountains or a lake, they can make you feel like you're there for a while."

"Virtual reality?"

"I don't know what you call it, but when I miss the Texas woodlands, I go there." Ruth turned in at a doorway, and they entered a small café bustling with activity and filled with the aroma of baking bread. "Would you like something?"

Still fearful of mind-altering drugs, Cassie refused. Ruth

made no comment, but her expression revealed a hint of humor as she helped herself to a cup of coffee and a brick-sized chocolate éclair. Leading the way to a small table, she made herself comfortable and waited for Cassie to do the same. "You really don't need to worry, darlin'. There's no agenda here except what Nancy told you."

Cassie snorted disdainfully. "That we're dead and she's trying to help us prepare for the next plane of existence? Really?" Ruth's brows rose, and she added, "How can you believe that?"

In answer, the woman stood, then bent and touched her palms to the floor. "See this?"

"That's pretty good," Cassie acknowledged.

Ruth sat down again, took a sip of her coffee, and hummed in appreciation. "When I was sixty-two, I started having problems getting around. At first it was just stiffness, but after while it got to be pain, the real kind that everyday medications don't touch. As time went on, I got more and more crippled, no matter what the doctors did." Her lips pulled in for a moment. "Believe me, they tried everything: drugs, therapy, surgery, and then more surgery. I went from being an active woman who loved to be outdoors to a twisted parody of a human being. I needed a cane, then a walker, then a wheelchair. For the last two years, I was pretty much confined to a bed."

"That's awful."

A harsh but probably unconscious glance from the old woman made Cassie blush, realizing she lacked any real understanding of pain and its long-term effects. Twenty-five and in excellent health, she couldn't possibly know how awful life had been for Ruth Waycliff. She'd seen her father struggle to breathe, but that wasn't like feeling it firsthand. Still, what else could a person say?

Ruth apparently understood. "I'm not telling this to get your sympathy. I'm telling it so you know why I believe I'm dead. Not only do I remember those last days, with my friends and family coming 'round to say goodbye, but I've got none of the pain I lived with all those years. I can move around, dance if I want to, and probably do push-ups if I wanted to show off." She looked down at herself. "This body may not look like much to you, but it works a whole lot better than what I had back there."

Cassie tried to reconcile what Ruth was claiming with reality. Perhaps the people in control of this place had given her some new drug, or maybe she'd been hypnotized into "remembering" a past life of pain. She was obviously pretty spry for an eighty-something, so her story was either a lie or a fantasy. Cassie got no sense that Ruth was lying, so she must have been brain-washed. Probably Rudy and the others were victims too. She'd have to determine how the brain-washing was done in order to avoid it. Still, she liked Ruth. It was nice to have someone to talk to, even if the person was delusional.

Ruth chatted amiably between bites, wiping smears of chocolate from her hands with a cloth napkin. Cassie learned she'd outlived three husbands, owned a ranch outside Austin that ran five hundred head of cattle, and had a passion for rescuing greyhounds. After twenty minutes with Ruth, Cassie knew more than she'd ever dreamed there was to know about dog care and feeding.

Finally, Ruth sat back and looked her in the eye. "Now it's your turn to talk."

A feeling of "I should have known" struck, although Ruth's expression revealed only interest and curiosity. Stubbornly Cassie resisted, kneading her own napkin absently. "Not much to tell."

Leaning back in her chair, Ruth ignored the blunt comment. "For me, death was a relief, and I was thrilled to find all this on the other side. For you, I suppose, it was quite a surprise."

"You might say that." *If it were true that I'm dead, which I'm not*, she added silently.

Ruth glanced at the doorway, where an attractive man greeted those who passed through. Cassie hadn't noticed him before, but he looked a lot like Orlando Bloom.

"I'll tell you what I told that Nancy person," Cassie said when Ruth turned back to her. "I don't know what the trick is, but I'm not falling for it, no matter what you or anyone else says."

"I know it's hard to accept that we've passed over—"

"Not hard," Cassie interrupted. "Impossible. I can't be dead. I can't be on some ship bound for Heaven or Eternity or Nirvana or whatever."

Ruth tried again. "Darlin', nobody wants to be dead, but isn't it comforting to know—"

Cassie stood, sending her chair skidding backward. "No. It isn't comforting to be told a fairy tale. I don't believe there's any kind of life after death! It's all garbage!" With that she left the room, passing the guy in the doorway without noticing that he turned to watch her go.

Pushing her way along the deck, Cassie returned to her stateroom and shut herself in, feeling doubly guilty. She'd been rude to Rudy, whose puppy-like eagerness didn't merit such treatment, and she'd hollered at Ruth, who was just a ditzy old lady. What was wrong with her?

No, she reprimanded herself. There was nothing wrong with her. It was this place, these people, who were wrong. She had to get away, but how? It was clever of them to keep their captives aboard a ship, because there was nowhere to run.

Once again, she wished she could talk to Christy. Her sister had always been there at home, waiting for Cassie's calls, visits, or confidences. What Cassie would give to talk to Christy now, or even to know where she was and what she was doing. She was probably a mess with no family left. No one else had ever mattered to Chris, and now Cassie feared her sister would be completely unable to function.

MUCH TO SEAMUS' RELIEF, Nordman decided to wrap up the

Parker case Thursday morning so he could concentrate on the body in Cambridge. When he rang the bell at Cassie Parker's apartment precisely at 9:00 a.m., Christy appeared in a hot pink, fuzzy robe, her eyes suspiciously red.

Taking in her disheveled appearance, Nordman said, "I can come back."

"No, please." She backed away, opening the door. Nordman stepped in but stopped in the entry area. Picking up on his reluctance, Christy said, "Have a seat. I'll be back in thirty seconds."

The estimate wasn't far off. She returned in a sweatshirt and flannel pants, her hair less rumpled and her face dewy from water she'd splashed on it. Taking the chair opposite Nordman at the kitchen table she asked, "What can you tell me?"

"Our investigation is complete." He cleared his throat and his voice took on an official tone. "What we call a 'view and report' was done rather than a complete autopsy." At Christy's questioning glance he explained, "When a case seems clearly accidental, we expedite things. Your sister died from a blow to the head caused by the guillotine set piece from the play. An accident."

Christy shivered but said politely, "I appreciate your coming by to tell me."

Nordman rose, already looking forward to the rest of his day. With one hand on the doorknob, he seemed to remember his empathy training. "Once again, we're sorry for your loss."

Seamus jumped to Christy as she trailed Nordman into the hallway. "Can I, um, arrange things now?"

The inspector put a hand to his forehead. "Sorry. I've got a lot on my mind and I've been feeling rough. The body will be released to whichever funeral home you choose."

Christy stood in the hallway, watching Nordman go. After he turned the corner, Seamus heard his footsteps quicken on the stairs, hurrying to get to the other case, the one that was clearly a homicide. Christy stayed where she was for a few moments, feeling abandoned. She went back into the apartment and closed the door before surrendering to another wave of grief.

Used to tears and recriminations, Seamus removed himself from Christy's, *Did I tell her I loved her when we spoke on the phone?* and *If I'd come straight to the theatre, would she still be alive?* It was the sort of thing the living tortured themselves with. Knowing life was finite, they pretended it went on forever. Daily refusal to acknowledge death's approach allowed humans to function, but it also left them unprepared for the end of life. He'd done the same thing in his lifetime, leaving important things unfinished and critical things unsaid.

As Christy cried out her tears, Seamus gleaned what he could about Cassie. Christy clearly had nothing to do with her sister's death, and she didn't know anyone at the Vic beyond polite introductions. He was pleased to discover, however, that she planned to go there today.

As Christy moved around getting ready to go out, Seamus surveyed the apartment: a kitchen-dining-living area, a bath, and a small, feminine bedroom. He filed away details in case he needed them to convince Cassie he'd actually been to her place.

There was evidence of a male presence in the apartment. It wasn't much: some toiletry articles, a pair of paint-spattered jeans and a sweatshirt, and a man's electric razor, all placed in a bag and set on the desk by the door. A masculine-looking leather jacket hung over the back of the desk chair. Recalling Nordman's notes, Seamus guessed the items belonged to the boyfriend she'd recently broken up with, the one who'd wronged her somehow. Cassie had no doubt meant to return them.

On the desk next to the bag was a yellow receipt, the old-fashioned kind that come in sets of two in a book, white for the business owner and yellow for the customer. It was from a garage in Malton, made out to Henry Spellman in scrawled handwriting. Across the lines meant for detailed accounting, it simply said, "Repairs—Prepaid—Cash." The paper was slightly crumpled, as if the customer had thrust it carelessly into a pocket, perhaps in the jacket on the chair. At least he'd learned the boyfriend's name.

CHRISTY SPENT MOST OF THE MORNING with a funeral director she'd located online. Following the directions given, she found the place, a long, low building with a discreet sign out front and a curved drive to facilitate a hearse's coming and going. The place was dimly lit and wood paneled, with thick carpeting to muffle footsteps, conversation, and, of course, sobs of grief. She was greeted immediately by the mortician. Unlike the dour fellow in Fairfield, this one was female, friendly, lively, and quite young.

"When would you like the service?" she asked as they sat at a refectory table.

"Cassie didn't want one. No funeral, immediate cremation, and no fuss, she said."

The woman nodded, looking slightly disappointed. Christy felt a little guilty, but it was her sister's wish. Besides, Cassie's accounts contained no money for an expensive funeral. Why would they? Her life had barely begun.

Christy left the mortuary a short time later with a small sense of accomplishment. She'd arranged things according to Cassie's wishes. When summer came, she'd hold a small memorial service before she placed the ashes in the family cemetery plot. It would make her feel she'd done something for her twin, and the customs of Fairfield would be adequately observed.

As she walked to the subway station, Christy took stock of the situation. Unable to sleep, she'd looked through Cassie's papers the night before, found her passwords, and tried to make a list of what she had to do. Cass had no outstanding bills and only a few recurring ones, like phone and Internet access. She'd been saddened by a number of notes from local agencies, thanking Cass for her help with various charity events. Her sister had loved helping others, especially children. Christy would send them all notification of Cassie's death.

She'd have little trouble settling Cassie's estate. When their father visited his lawyer to make a will, the girls had decided they might as well do the same. Dad left everything to them, and Cassie and Christy had willed what they had to each other. Christy now owned the family farm in Fairfield, a pickup truck, a middle-aged Toyota RAV4, and Cassie's tiny store of cash.

The farm was rented out to a man who planted rotating crops each spring and paid them enough in fall to cover the taxes. The house was home, but Christy felt little desire to return there. She'd watched her father die in that old house on a little-traveled road, and it seemed at present a place with too many bad memories.

She couldn't think of anyone in Fairfield who'd care, really care, about Cassie's death. Their school friends were all involved in their own lives: husbands and wives, children and jobs. An obituary in the local paper would bring surprise and shock, but nobody in Fairfield would actually miss Cassie. She'd been gone too long for that.

If she was honest, few would notice if Christy Parker never returned, either. Her preoccupation with Earl's illness had led her to withdraw from most things, and life had filled whatever small holes her absence made in Fairfield's daily routines. As if the conclusion had been in her mind all along, waiting for her to notice it, Christy realized that Fairfield was her past. She wanted something different, something challenging. She boarded the subway train, took a seat, and gazed out the window. As it began its gentle bump and sway, she realized she wanted to stay in Toronto and see what it offered for her future.

Chapter Six

CHRISTY'S NEXT STOP WAS AT THE THEATRE, to pick up the suitcase she'd left there. Becoming more familiar with the subway system, she easily figured out how to get to the Vic from the funeral home and, as a bonus, encountered no more perverts. It was just after twelve when she arrived, and the front doors opened with an easy pull and a whoosh of air.

The lobby was dimly lit by a row of lights suspended from the ceiling, and the posters on the wall were less impressive without the track lights that highlighted them during performances. At the ticket booth she found a woman sorting envelopes into alphabetical order. After identifying herself, Christy asked where her suitcase might be.

"I think Neen put it in his office. Go into the auditorium and turn left. You'll see it along the back wall." Her hand reached out, though Christy was too far away to touch. "I'm really sorry about Cassie."

Thanking her, Christy entered the auditorium. Once inside the double doors, she stopped for a moment, feeling like an interloper. She'd been there before, of course, but always with Cass.

The building had sat abandoned for years before the current director bought it, removed the outdated machinery, and renovated. At the front were the lobby, restrooms, and offices. The central area, open to the roof, was the auditorium with rows of increasingly raised seats. Above them an old loft had been made into a balcony and more restrooms. Above that, ancient storerooms had been cleared of clutter and converted to living quarters for the director, Albert Somebody.

At the back of the building, behind the stage, the old factory floor was used for storage, sets, stage equipment, and dressing rooms. There were two large rooms where most of the actors changed and four closet-sized rooms for the headliners. Christy had glimpsed one in passing, noting there was barely room for a dressing table, a sink, a clothes rack, and a couple of chairs. Still, they were private. The stars of the troupe did not have to disrobe in front of the part-timers and the students.

Above the backstage area was a second loft, used for wardrobe creation and storage. Reached by a staircase near the rear entrance to the building, the loft's deck ended a few feet above the cyclorama curtain. Leaning on a wrought-iron railing that ran along the edge, Christy and Cassie had sometimes watched the actors below during rehearsals, Cassie commenting about this one or that as they laughed together.

Everything had been easier with her sister to lean on. Even when they weren't together, when Cass was reaching for what she wanted and Chris was telling herself she didn't want anything, they'd had each other to talk to. Now it was different. Her sister's death made Christy realize that pursuing what she wanted now, not later, was vital. She'd willingly delayed decisions about her life, but it was time to act, to decide who Christy Parker was besides Cassie's sister and Earl's daughter.

A noise from somewhere ahead of her brought her back to her purpose. There were two doors; the first was closed and said "Technician." The second was open, revealing filing cabinets, posters, and stacks of boxes with names scribbled on the sides: *Oliver, Earnest,* and *Pinafore.* The door's lettering said *Gunnini, Manager.*

Christy knocked tentatively.

"Yeah?" came a voice.

She stepped into the room but saw no one. A moment later, a tousled head appeared from the side of the desk. "Oh!" The head disappeared briefly then a man rose like a jack-in-the-box. "Sorry, I thought you were Donna." He wiped a hand on his jeans and extended it. "Carl Gunnini, usually known as Neen. You have to be Christy." He went to a corner and retrieved her suitcase. "No doubt you came for this."

"Thanks," she told him. "Sorry I forgot it before."

"You had a lot on your mind." He didn't quite meet her eyes and abruptly switched topics. "Cassie talked about you all the time."

"You and my sister were close?"

"Yeah. I liked her a lot. My wife did too," he added, apparently anxious to prevent any mistaken conclusions. "Cass helped out around here with more than just costumes. His expression turned sad. "She was really a good person. When we did charity stuff at the schools and even at the prison, she was always the first one to volunteer to help, and—"

"Neen, are you in there?" The voice outside the door was a resonating baritone. A second later, a man smaller than his voice indicated appeared in the doorway. "Oh. I didn't know you had company."

"Albert, this is Cassie's sister, Christine."

Before she knew it, she was swept into an embrace of masculine arms and heady cologne. "Dear girl. I am so sorry!"

"Thanks," she mumbled into a cashmere shoulder.

When she could breathe again, Neen said, "Albert Marle, our director and lead actor."

Christy recalled seeing Marle at least twice before in shows her sister costumed. Well into middle age, he was a handsome specimen with sleek, dark hair. His rather slight stature had probably kept him from playing lead roles in his heyday, but he had the kind of smile that seemed electric, emitting jolts of personality into the room.

"It's nice to meet you, Mr. Marle."

"We all loved Cassie," he said, abandoning the smile momentarily in deference to her grief. "She didn't take any guff, but she was the best costumer I've ever worked with."

"She said Christy was just as good." Hearing a note in Neen's voice, Christy turned toward him.

"No way. I mean, I sewed for people back home, but—"

Marle looked at her speculatively. "I think Neen is attempting to broach a subject we've been grappling with." He took a dramatic pose, leaning toward her with hands out in supplication. "Miss Parker, would you consider undertaking your sister's job?"

"What? No! I'm studying business. I've only had a few design classes, nothing like the theatrical costume course of study Cass had." She was babbling, and she knew it.

Neen came out from behind his desk, joining Marle. "The timing is terrible, we realize that, but we're in a bind. *Two Cities* ends in three weeks. Cass was working on the costumes for a Dickens revue, with bits from his stories put to music."

Marle took Christy's hand as if unwilling to let her go. "We have her drawings, and she'd done most of the purchasing. We need someone who can pull it all together."

She fidgeted with the suitcase handle. "Surely there are seamstresses available."

"Not as many as you'd think," Neen replied. "Cassie often

said you were every bit as good as she—" Stuck on a choice between *is* and *was*, Neen left the sentence unfinished.

Christy took a step back. "I can't believe we're talking about this. My sister just died."

Both men turned apologetic. "Of course," Neen said. "It's wrong of us to bring it up."

Marle put a hand on her shoulder. "We're sorry. Really. It's just that we're a little desperate. Three weeks isn't very long."

"Stop it, Albert," Neen ordered. "We're out of line."

Marle shook himself as if trying to get it into his head. "I am truly sorry for your loss."

Christy bit her lip. They did seem sorry. And desperate. A job offer when she had just this morning decided to stay in Toronto. Could things simply fall into place so easily?

No. She could not make a decision this way, just because someone said they needed her. "I'm going to stay in Cassie's apartment for a few days, then I'll probably go home."

She handed Neen one of the cards Cassie had insisted on ordering for her. She hadn't handed out a single one in Fairfield, where everyone already knew where she lived and could look up her phone number in the ridiculously skinny phone book. Here they seemed useful and natural, making her feel like a capable individual rather than the clerk at Grocery Mart. She was someone you might need to contact, someone with something to offer.

"If you do decide to stay on—" At a look from Neen, Marle stopped.

"Really, I couldn't." Picking up the suitcase, Christy started out. She knew better than to think she could do Cassie's job. Didn't she?

At the door she turned to find that the men had followed, as if reluctant to let her escape. A feeling, maybe confidence, maybe madness, rose in her. "I'll think about it."

Marle let out a sigh, and she guessed he was relieved their proposal hadn't been rejected out of hand. "Thank you, Miss Parker. Again, please accept our condolences."

"You could come to the show tonight and watch what happens backstage," Neen suggested. "It might help you decide if you'd like to be part of this circus."

She thought about that. It was odd, given the circumstances, but what else did she have to do? As a matter of fact, what did she have to do with the rest of her life?

"I guess I could."

She left the office, turning her face away from the stage and trying not to dwell on the fact that not far away, her last living relative had died, suddenly and tragically.

THAT AFTERNOON Cassie again ventured onto the deck, which appeared to be sun-lit even without a sun overhead. The ship seemed to float in a bright bubble, and beyond the rail was that beautiful, engaging, and peace-inducing something. She tried not to look directly at it, figuring it was some sort of magnetic imaging that worked on the brain to create a soporific effect.

It was unnerving, walking along such a normal-yet-abnormal deck in such a comfortable-yet-uncomfortable situation. She was relieved when she spotted Ruth sitting in a chair near one of the swimming pools. A novel lay overturned on her lap, and she gazed at the colors in the distance, an expression of serenity on her face. Seeing Cassie, Ruth called out, "Join me, Yankee Girl."

Instinct said this woman was not out to deceive her. If tricks were involved, Ruth was a victim, not a perpetrator. "I'm sorry I was a brat before," Cassie began, dragging a deck chair next to Ruth's with a bumpy scrape. "It's just—"Cassie sat down. "I don't know what to believe."

"I understand that," the older woman replied. Raising both hands, palms out, she said, "Until I met you, I'd have said an atheist would be the one kind of person I'd never meet on this ship."

"That's why it can't—" Cassie stopped. If the old woman wanted to believe she was on her way to heaven, who was she to dissuade her? If they'd pumped her full of drugs, reason would do no good.

Avoiding the topic of being or not being dead, she encouraged Ruth to talk about her life: her children, her home, Texas. Ruth talked willingly, taking responsibility for the conversation as Cassie listened. Oddly, Ruth relayed all kinds of information about Texas but seemed fuzzy on details about her family. *Maybe dementia*, Cassie thought when the woman couldn't name two of her own children.

Ruth rubbed her forehead, frustrated, and Cassie looked away to give her a moment. The temperature was perfect. She was warm but not the least bit sweaty, and the breeze that ruffled her hair was ever so gentle. Perfect conditions. Perfect.

Shaking her head in disgust, Ruth gave up the quest for her daughters' names and squirmed to a more comfortable position. "They'll come if I let my brain work on it, I suppose." She turned to Cassie. "Tell me about Toronto."

"Well, I worked at a theatre there, making costumes."

Ruth clapped her hands. "I did love the theatre! What kinds of things did you make?"

Cassie explained the Victorian theme of the company and mentioned some characters she thought Ruth would recognize, like Tiny Tim and the pirates of Penzance.

"What an interesting job! I'll bet you got to meet lots of famous people."

"Our troupe is mostly actors on the way up or the way down, if you know what I mean. The really good young ones will soon move on to bigger theatres. Older actors come to us when they want to stop traveling or want something less strenuous than Stratford, where they often play three roles at a time. Our schedule is less hectic: a show's on for three weeks, a week off, and we start a new show."

"Sensible, I'd say." Ruth raised thin, white brows. "What about the rest of it? Family?"

"My father died just a few weeks ago after a long illness.

My twin sister was coming to the city to visit me on Thursday." She glanced around, her anxiety returning. "That's why I need to get back. She must be worried sick."

Ruth's head made a tiny negative movement, but she only asked, "Any special man in your life?"

She looked away. "Not anymore."

Ruth's interest was piqued. "You recently broke up with a boyfriend?"

Cassie paused. The people at the Vic knew why she and Henry had split. Cassie hadn't told Christy about it, believing she had enough grief and didn't need to hear about Cassie's romantic troubles. There could be no harm in telling this interested almost-stranger the whole story.

"In Dad's last days, I went home to be with him. Henry and I were fine when I left Toronto, and when Dad died, he even came to the funeral." Cassie moved slightly in her chair. "He only drove up for the service, and he left in time to make the evening performance, but that was okay. In fact, it was good. Christy and I only have each other now, and with Henry there I felt like I was leaving her out, you know?"

"You and your sister were close."

Cassie gave her a look. "Yes. We are." Ruth didn't react, and she went on. "When I got back to Toronto, things had changed. I went to the theatre last Tuesday to work on a costume that had been damaged. I was at the back of the women's dressing room, certainly not hiding, but not in plain sight, and I heard Henry talking to one of the actresses, Kim Snyder. I only got part of it, but I heard enough to learn the two of them had spent a night together at an inn somewhere."

"Oh, no!"

Cassie shrugged, trying to appear—trying to *be* casual about Henry's betrayal. "I'm okay with it now, but at that moment, it hit me like an army tank. I started to cry, and I had to get out of there. I tried to be quiet, but I was all messed up, bawling and angry and hurt. I ran out of the theatre without knowing where I was going. I just wanted to be away from him." She paused, reliving the scene. "It was storming like mad, and there I was, sobbing in the alley and making a fool of myself." The emotions she'd felt that day returned, and tears formed at the corners of her eyes.

"I've always had trouble imagining a northern winter." Ruth's interruption was clearly a ploy to give Cassie a chance to recover. "I've experienced snow, the crunch of it underfoot, the chill in the air, the biting wind. But living through it for months on end! I've never been able to grasp that."

"It's great." Cassie made a comic grimace, still blinking back tears. "Anyway, Henry came after me." Warming to her subject, Cassie turned her gaze to the colors in the distance and watched the soft lights dance. Let them hypnotize her if they could! Maybe she'd forget how she'd felt that morning.

She spoke to the colors, feeling Ruth's interest but speaking for herself. "He insisted I'd misunderstood, but I hadn't and I knew it." Her voice dropped. "Just Kim's tone of voice was enough to indicate a change in their relationship. She ordered him around like they were an old married couple: "Don't say this" and "Remember that.""

"Don't say what?"

"I guess they were trying to cover up the fact they'd been together." Cassie sniffed, wiping her still-wet eyes. "As if anyone except me cared what those two did."

Ruth returned her to the story. "What did your young man say in his defense?"

"The usual stuff. It was just a mistake. It wouldn't happen again. He loved me, not her. I told him to save his breath."

"Then what did you do?"

Cassie ran a hand through her short curls. "I realized I'd been sleeping with a liar and a cheat." Her lips pulled into a tight line. "The only way to deal with a guy like that is to cut him out of your life. I told him we were done."

"Oh." Ruth sounded faintly disappointed, as if she'd hoped Cassie had punched Henry in the nose. "Then what happened?"

"I was a mess, crying and shivering with cold. I honestly think he felt bad, though Henry seldom realizes that other people have feelings."

"It sounds like you were better off without him."

Cassie bit her lip. "I wasn't in love with him, but he was funny and good-looking, and he took my mind off things. If my dad hadn't just died—I don't know."

"So how did it end?"

"Oh, he was all concern for me. He said I was going to freeze out there and tried to put his arm around me. When I shrugged him off, he realized his famous charm wasn't going to work this time. He took off his jacket and put it around my shoulders." Unconsciously she pantomimed her reaction, fists to chest as if closing the coat around herself. "He asked if we could talk when I was calmer; I said no. Talking couldn't fix what he'd done. Then he said, 'Cass, I'm really sorry.'"

Cassie turned to Ruth, rubbing a hand across her brow as if erasing her emotion. "I told him I was going home for a while, but I'd be back for the performance. Before I walked away, I said, 'Henry, don't ever speak to me again.'" She smiled grimly. "I've avoided him—and her—ever since."

Once again, Cassie could tell what was on Ruth's mind by her bland expression. If what they'd tried to tell her for two days was true, she'd never have to worry about facing Kim Snyder or Henry Spellman again.

Chapter Seven

As Christy left The Vic, Seamus jumped to Neen, the theatre manager, and within a short time learned that the man's job description might read, "Do everything." Neen saw to the stage, the bookkeeping, the advertising, and the actors, jollying those along who needed it and gently bullying those who didn't pull their weight. The Vic was a small but professional operation, and glances Seamus got of reviews posted on the office wall indicated respect from the critics. That did not, of course, translate into wealth. The troupe barely squeaked by, and every member of the company knew that economy was the watchword, not out front where the audience could see it, but anywhere else it could be achieved. He suspected that was why Neen and Marle wanted Christy, an amateur, to finish her sister's work.

Everyone helped with staging. Each actor was charged with carrying on or off various props and set pieces while a two-man crew handled the larger sets. Neen apparently insisted they practice until scene changes were fast and efficient. Set pieces, which were brought on from the left and taken off to the right, were stacked neatly backstage in designated spots so that next time they were needed, it was a simple matter to locate them. Long delays made an audience restless, and even though the current production was well underway, Neen still spent time trying to find ways to speed things up.

Seamus found the activity backstage more interesting than watching from the audience. He'd liked the theatre well enough the few times he went; it just wasn't something he chose to do. Backstage was different, though, like looking into the workings of a clock. The onstage world had to be carefully planned, and he listened with interest as Neen thought about a dozen things at once.

That evening, about an hour before the play, Neen noticed Christy standing uncertainly before the apron. Hurrying down the steps, he took her hand. "I'm glad you came," he said, leading her to the stage wing. "Sit here, and you can see everything without getting in anyone's way."

The space, between the proscenium arch and the inside

wall, put her out of the traffic pattern of actors' entrances and exits. Neen pointed at a battered stool. "When we start a new production, someone sits there to cue actors who forget a line or relay reports from the back of the theatre about what the audience can hear and see. Now that *Two Cities* has been running for a while, there isn't much call for that, or for wardrobe help, either. Donna's been handling what there is of it."

Seamus had learned that the female at the ticket window who looked fourteen was actually a woman in her thirties. She was also Neen's wife.

Neen pointed to a table behind them. "Here's one thing Cassie did before every show. Some characters have specific items that go with their costumes, and they keep track of those. But for general use, we share gloves and fans and such, so they're left out on this table. Some of the actors aren't as good as they should be about returning them, so she kept track of it."

"I see." Christy sounded slightly overwhelmed, and Seamus wondered if she would ever have the confidence to take the position she'd been offered. Two family deaths, a new and possibly high-pressure job. If she did sign on at

The Vic, Christy would leave her past behind in a big way.

Neen's concern was for the here and now. "The other thing Cass did during performances was mend costumes if something happened to them. A skirt catches on a nail and tears, or a zipper breaks, or someone loses a stocking. Those are things the wardrobe mistress takes care of."

"I see." After a beat she asked, "Where's the kit?"

"The what?" Neen looked perplexed.

"The sewing kit. There would be a box or something with stuff for making repairs." It sounded like Christy had made a decision, and Seamus felt a rush of relief in Neen's mind.

"I don't know," he said, "but Donna will."

They went to find Donna, who indeed knew about the sewing kit. "Cassie had two," she told Christy, "a small one she kept with her and a larger one back here." She led the way to a spot in the wings where an overhead shelf held an old Easter basket filled with all sorts of sewing notions. On top of it was a black fanny-pack with items useful for temporary mending: elastic, plain buttons, scissors, needles of several sizes and threads of many colors.

Christy took the fanny pack when she returned to her corner of the stage, which pleased Neen, though like

Seamus, he wondered if she was capable of doing what her more confident sister had so effortlessly done. Seamus heard his thought: *She hasn't got Cassie's spirit, just a desire to be helpful.*

Backstage was stirring, and actors moved back and forth in various stages of dress. Marle appeared and began circulating, giving bits of direction but also touching each person he spoke to. Donna brought out the larger sewing kit and went to work on a tall, attractive woman whose corset button had come off. As her husband passed, Donna asked him, "Do you think she's going to stay?"

"I think so." It was Neen's way, Seamus guessed, to assure others that things would be all right.

"Good, because I'm not the one to be doing this."

As if to confirm it, the woman yelped, "Ow! You poked me!"

"If you hadn't put on weight, you wouldn't be bursting your buttons, Kim."

"I haven't put on one ounce," the girl replied sulkily. "Cassie made it too tight. She was always doing stuff like that to me."

"Yeah, right. And you never did anything to her." Donna

rolled her eyes at her husband, but he was already moving on.

As he crossed the stage, Neen looked up at the guillotine that was an integral part of the play's final scene. It was firmly affixed to the wall, as it should have been the day Cassie died. Obviously it hadn't been secured properly the night before. That meant someone hadn't done his job.

Neen had avoided confronting the two young actors with the fact that their carelessness had probably led to Cassie's death, but he told himself, *Got to address the issue sooner or later.*

"Josh, Randy, can I see you for a minute?"

The two looked at each other and warily followed Neen to an empty area at the back. They were dressed as French footmen, in elaborately decorated uniforms. One had dark hair and eyes, with the look of a poet, while the other was blond and athletic-looking, with the upper-body strength and muscular legs of a wrestler.

The stage manager spoke softly but with purpose. "We need to talk about the guillotine."

The blond one, apparently the more vocal of the two, began his argument. "Neen, we told the police. The damned thing was put away exactly like it's supposed to be."

"Yeah," the dark-haired one added. "The straps were tight. Josh tried it, like he always does."

"I did," Josh agreed. "Randy secures it, and then I always make sure it's going to stay put."

Neen sighed. "All right. Just be more careful in the future." It was a dumb thing to say, Seamus thought. If these guys had indeed neglected their job, it was too late to prevent catastrophe now.

He thought about jumping to one of the men Neen held responsible for the accident, but the show would begin soon, and they would be focused on playing their parts. Neen was a better source of information for now, since he circulated constantly among cast and crew. Besides, Seamus had picked up worry in Neen's mind regarding Christy and Albert Marle. It wasn't clear why, but the manager was hoping their director stayed away from their new and rather innocent wardrobe mistress.

Seamus was able to meet most of the company as Neen spoke to the sound crew, the lights manager, the lead actors, and Marle, now dressed as Jarvis Lorry in a dark frock coat and shiny top hat. As actors passed, some in full makeup, others less ready, Neen joked with them, encouraged them, and reminded them of small matters important to them individually. Seamus noticed he called them by their character names, no doubt helping to mentally prepare them for their roles.

"Lucy," he told the lead actress, a beautiful blonde whose innocent face was framed by a heart-shaped bonnet, "Try to be a little more tearful when you find your long-lost father."

She gave him a look unsuited to sweet Lucy Manette. "Tell the old goat to stop pinching my ass whenever I get close, and I'll try to be more sympathetic."

Neen dutifully went to find Ted, an aging actor whose makeup made him seem haggard and gaunt, as one who'd spent years in a French prison would be. "Dr. Manette, you've got to keep your hands off Lucy. She's going to file a complaint with the union." Apparently in Neen's experience, simply asking would get him nowhere with Ted.

"An accident, Neen. When I lean on Tarcie, I sometimes happen to touch her behind."

Neen sighed. "Well, don't let it 'happen' again. Dr. Manette can lean on Jarvis Lorry."

As he turned away, Seamus noticed Kim, repairs to her

costume completed, watching the exchange with sardonic humor. She said something to another actress, Kim's best friend in the company. Neen corrected himself: *Her only friend.*

Kim smirked as Neen passed. "Good luck getting that old creep to behave himself."

Neen smiled, but Seamus sensed dislike. "Makeup looks good, Miss Pross."

Actually, makeup was amazing. When Seamus first saw the girl, she'd been a pretty brunette with olive skin and dark eyes. Now her skin looked pasty, she had wrinkles around her eyes and mouth, and her hair was streaked with gray. Severe black garments flattened and widened her figure. She looked every bit the middle-aged spinster who served as Lucy Manette's constant companion. He wondered if Kim liked playing the role, which, though meaty, hid her attractiveness. He guessed not.

"Amy, speed up your costume change," Neen said to the other woman, whose youthful prettiness was hidden by blacked-out teeth, a frizzy wig, and clothing that was little more than rags. "I know it's tough to get from Paris to London quickly, but we need people on the streets in both cities." From that Seamus guessed Amy was one of the nameless characters who filled in scenes.

"I try," she whined, "but it's hard to go from dirty to pretty in a few seconds."

Everyone else manages, Neen thought, but he said aloud, "Try harder." Amy gave a noncommittal murmur, and Seamus guessed that as soon as the manager's back was turned, there would be mutual eye-rolling between her and Kim.

Fifteen minutes before curtain time, the actors assembled on the stage, dressed and ready for the show but with an air that something else would come before. When everyone was there, Neen and Albert took places near the front, and the noise level, muted anyway in deference to the audience gathering a few feet away, ceased altogether.

"We're dedicating this show to Cassie," Neen announced quietly. "She didn't want a funeral or anything, but we want to recognize her dedication and her spirit." He took a candle from his pocket, and Seamus saw that the others had them too. Josh stepped forward and lit Neen's candle with his lighter. At the same time, Randy lit the candle Albert held. The two men then lit the candles of cast and crew members until the dark stage glowed with dozens of tiny lights.

"Cassie, we will miss you," Albert said.

From somewhere in the back Seamus heard Donna's voice. "And we love you."

Several voices echoed that sentiment, and the candles rose together in a salute. "To Cassie." After a few seconds of silence, Albert lowered his light and blew it out, head bowed. The others did the same, and then the group melted away, each to his task. The show must go on. Life goes on.

Seamus knew Christy Parker was watching from her corner, and he was glad Neen didn't glance her way. He was sure the girl from Fairfield didn't want anyone to see the tears she shed in the dark.

CASSIE STOOD LOOKING over the ship's rail, judging the distance to whatever was below. After she'd stared at it for some time, she sensed a presence and turned her head slightly. A man stood a few feet away, one she'd noticed several times now because he looked so much like Orlando Bloom.

"What?"

"I'm not a stalker," he said, showing his palms in surrender, "but you are on my watch list."

"Watch list?"

He glanced down. "If you go over the side, you're a lost soul, and we won't be able to help you."

"Yeah, right." She sounded childish, even to her own ears.

He held up a hand. "You don't believe us. I get that, and I never argue with a client."

Cassie rolled her eyes. "I'm not your client. And I am not staying here. Sooner or later, I'll find a way to escape, and then you'll face the consequences of kidnapping all these people and arranging this huge scam. You'll have to answer to the authorities for all this."

"Cassie, we only answer to one authority."

"I know what you're going to say, and you might as well save your breath. I will never believe a word you say, you or Nancy or Rudy or anyone here." She turned and stalked away, struggling to maintain her anger. The man's presence, like the aura outside the ship, summoned something from inside her. If she let it, Cassie suspected she would succumb to a sense of peace. No matter how they did it, with drugs or whatever, there was no way she'd fall for it.

LESS THAN TEN MINUTES after their solemn farewell to Cassie, the company was back to the business of creating entertainment. Neen glanced at his watch and called, "Places!" Within a few seconds, there was a change in lighting, a darkening beyond the curtain, and low lights on the stage. As music played out front, the actors set the opening scene, moving to their assigned spots and taking head-down poses, as if asleep standing up.

Neen stepped behind the sets and raised a hand, signaling the time had come. Soon the music ended, and Albert Marle's voice came over the sound system, welcoming the audience and, as was necessary these days, asking them to turn off cell phones. Neen peered around the half-lit stage as the announcement received polite applause. When he was sure everything was ready, he backed away and signaled the crew. The curtain rose.

Once she recovered from the emotion of the tribute to her sister, Christy allowed herself to become immersed in *A Tale of Two Cities*. She watched intently, fascinated by her strikingly different perspective. From her corner she saw the on-stage action, but she also saw the rest of it: the faces of the actors as they waited for their entrance cues, the "let-down" look as they left the stage and resumed their own personalities again, the scrambling at odd moments when things didn't go as planned. Mrs. Cruncher forgot to bring her prayer book on stage and had to change a line to account for it. A man at Madame Defarge's shop, one of the many Jacques, jumped ahead a few lines, skipping an important revelation. The woman playing the murderous knitter, obviously an old hand, casually slipped the line into a later speech.

The mistakes made little difference to Christy, who only picked them up from whispered comments among the actors. The play was riveting, the actors well suited to their parts. Having seen them earlier as themselves, she thought she'd have a hard time accepting them in their roles, but the spell of the theatre made her forget it was pretense. She became lost, first in Paris, then in London, more than two hundred years in the past.

That is, until a youth playing the role of young Jerry Cruncher, son of the unrepentant grave-robber, hurried up to her. "Are you the wardrobe lady?"

"Um—" Christy felt her whole life had come down to this question. Was she the grocery clerk visiting from the sticks, or was she a part of the show, one of them?

The boy didn't wait for an answer. "I split my pants, and I'm in the next scene."

She looked around. Donna was at the back of the stage, helping a woman change costumes. Opening the kit she'd left on the floor beside her, Christy ordered, "Turn around. I'll see what I can do."

By the time the performance was over, Christy considered herself part of the company. She'd helped with costume adjustments, located props, and even figured out how to speed up costume changes for Amy and some of the other characters. "If I bring some of the costumes to the space under the stairs at a certain point," she told Neen, "actors will save the time it takes to get to the dressing room and back to the stage."

"That would help with the shifts from Paris to London," Neen said, eyeing the spot thoughtfully.

"We could put up a curtain," she said, demonstrating with her arms where a drape might hang. "To provide privacy while they change."

"Actors learn not to worry much about privacy," Neen said with a chuckle. "But that's a great idea. And I saw you helping Jerry out. Thanks."

She shrugged. "If it's going to be my job, I figured I might as well jump in."

Neen put a hand on Christy's arm. "I'm really glad you're willing to give this a try. Tomorrow, Donna and I can show you what we're going to need for *Definitely Dickens.*"

She swallowed, awed at the magnitude of what she was agreeing to. "Okay."

"Let's meet here at ten." He frowned, and a single curl fell onto his forehead. "Is that too early?"

She was usually up at six, at work by eight. "Ten's fine."

"I think you'll like wardrobe," Neen said. "Helping backstage is good, but if you're a creative type, you'll be happiest up there, where making the new costumes is all up to you."

Christy didn't know whether she was terrified or ecstatic. People often said she was creative, but that didn't mean she was ready for such a large step. As panic threatened, she heard her father's voice as if he spoke inside her head.

"Parts."

That had been her dad's philosophy for dealing with life. A man of few words, he would say when she was stressed, "Parts, Chris. Break a difficult job into parts." Once when his mood was expansive, he'd explained the mantra in terms of his own work. "Running a farm is complicated. There are always big jobs that take weeks or months, small jobs to be done every day, and surprise jobs that appear when you least want them, like a cow that has trouble in labor or a broken tractor. It could be overwhelming if a guy thought about it all at once."

He'd pushed his cap back, exposing the white strip across his forehead that the sun never reached. "The trick is to break it down, decide what you can do today, what you should think about for tomorrow, and what you just can't worry about right now." He'd smiled, adding, "Your mother's old friend St. Francis had the best advice there is: handle what you can, accept that there are things you can't handle, at least not now or by yourself, and figure out the difference between the two."

That was what she would have to do if she took on Cassie's job: break it down into parts that she could manage, do what she could do each day, and try not to worry about whether she could do it as well as Cass would have. What more could they ask of her?

"You'll be a fine wardrobe mistress, Miss Parker," said a voice behind her. Christy turned to see Albert Marle, still in costume with mutton-chop whiskers and a fake paunch. "I intend to take a personal interest in you."

Christy felt a shiver go down her spine. She had an exciting new job that would test her skills and make use of her talents. She would be living in a city that offered all kinds of possibilities. And she was going to be part of something colorful, interesting, and exciting. Something she already knew she loved.

SEAMUS FELT PART OF THE NIGHT'S theatrical success as he hosted with the stage crew. He watched as Len worked the light board. He spent time with Martin, the sound tech, who made sure everyone had a microphone and adjusted the levels so the audience neither strained to hear nor winced in aural pain. Seamus had never thought about the fact that some actors' voices carried better than others, but the sound crew had to be aware of it and make adjustments. Hosting with Wayne, a member of the set crew, he saw the clever tricks that made scenery manageable: hidden wheels, panels that flipped, and hollow pieces that weighed next to nothing but looked substantial from a distance.

Jumping from actor to crew member to actor again, Seamus learned little more about the case than he already knew. The shock of Cassie's death was wearing off, as such things do for all but those closest to the victim. He learned about the recent break-up between Cassie and Henry Spellman. People had been surprised when Henry took up with Kim, but they generally didn't think about it too much. Henry was not known for thinking of others, and Kim was universally disliked although undeniably attractive.

Curious, Seamus spent a few minutes with Henry. He was focused on his role and almost single-mindedly devoted to excellence at his craft, which was admirable. If Henry was a louse where women were concerned, as Donna thought he was, it didn't seem to bother him much. He was sorry Cassie was dead, but his thoughts, when he had a few moments outside his character, were about Kim, who he found sexy, smart, and a little dangerous, much more exciting than the pragmatic Cassie.

Any fleeting thoughts Henry had that might be construed as guilt were connected to Albert Marle. If Seamus got the idea, and he wasn't sure he did, Spellman had cheated Albert somehow. He felt mildly guilty about it, but he was mostly concerned with keeping Albert from finding out. Seamus wanted to know if Albert knew about Henry's secret, and he also wondered why Neen was concerned about Albert and Christy.

Seamus continued his travels as Spellman went back on as Charles Darnay, jumping from actor to actor and listening for thoughts about Cassie. The only thing of interest he picked up came from a young actor named Ben who'd been in the theatre just before Cassie died. He'd come to retrieve his wallet, stashed under the frame of the fainting couch and forgotten the day before. There'd been no one in the building, but he knew, as many did, that with a little effort, a person could jump up, catch hold of the fire escape ladder at the back of the building, climb it, and get in through an upstairs window that had no lock. As Ben made his way across the dark stage, he'd heard movement at the front. When no further noise followed, he'd concluded he was mistaken, located his wallet, and left.

Ben hadn't mentioned his break-in to the police, because it was technically illegal. His principal thought was that luck had been with him. The unsecured guillotine had not come loose when he took the same route across the stage that Cassie must have taken a few minutes later.

Chapter Eight

IN NANCY'S OFFICE THE NEXT MORNING Cassie said, "I'd like to propose a compromise."

Nancy raised her eyes to Cassie's. "What sort of compromise?"

"If you really want me to believe I'm dead, let me talk to my father." She thought it was pretty clever. If they couldn't produce her dad, they'd have to admit to trying to trick her. A strange thought niggled at the back of her mind: *And if I am dead, at least I can see him and know that he's okay.*

She pushed that thought away as a regretful expression formed on Nancy's face. Cassie hurried on. "I understand people can stay here as long as they want, enjoying the food and all the things they can do. It hasn't been that long, and I'll bet my dad is still here. Just check your records." She looked around for any sign of recordkeeping, but there was no computer, no filing cabinet, not even a telephone. She heard her own voice turn plaintive. "It would mean a lot to me.”

“We don’t allow reunions,” Nancy said. “You must understand; there are just too many factors we can’t control in such meetings.”

Cassie lowered her head, staring at her hands as they twisted in her lap. Desperation bubbled to the surface. She’d been selfish! She could see that now, but she could no longer change it. She’d thought only of her own happiness, had done only what she wanted. She’d never thought about Christy, left on the farm with a dead-end job and their dying father.

“I need to go home.”

Nancy’s voice was kind but firm. “It’s not possible, Cassie.”

“Christy’s got no one but me.”

“She will go on. She’ll have to.”

“She needs me.” Cassie leaned forward earnestly. “Christy hangs back too much, afraid she’ll bother somebody or cause a fuss. I plan to move her to Toronto with me so she’ll come out of her shell a little bit.” She added with a pleading note, “It’ll only take a few months.”

Nancy met her gaze. “Your life is over, Cassie. Your

sister's will go on without you."

THE MORNING AFTER her first back-stage experience, Christy started making coffee in her sister's kitchen and found herself sobbing before the brew was half done. Seamus, who'd jumped to her from Neen the night before, waited patiently for her to recover, understanding how grief can return without warning when life seems to have returned to normal.

That sense of normalcy, and even a bit of anticipation, returned in time. Christy dried her tears and headed to the shower, determined to make the day productive. Donning jeans, a sweatshirt, shoes, and a jacket, she was almost ready to leave when a hesitant knock came on the door. Opening it, she found Henry Spellman standing there, looking boyish and uncomfortable.

"Miss Parker. I'm sorry to bother you so early in the morning, but I—I left some things here." His smile was disarming. "I thought you might start packing things up, and I'd hate to lose my stuff."

He'd apparently missed the news that she was The Vic's

new wardrobe mistress. "Please, come in." Christy pointed to a bag of items on the desk. "Cass had some things laid out."

"It's my stuff," he said, checking the bag.

"And is this your jacket too?"

"Yes. I loaned it to her one day when it was cold." He took a breath that sounded close to a sob. "I can't believe she's gone." Tears formed in his eyes, but he blinked them back. "We'd had some trouble recently, but I hoped we'd be able to get back together."

"What kind of trouble?" Things had been all right between them when Henry left Fairfield. They must have quarreled soon after Cassie returned to Toronto.

He shrugged and shook his head at once, giving a mixed signal. "A misunderstanding; that's all. If we'd had a chance to talk it through, we'd have been okay."

Christy didn't ask for details, though Seamus knew she wanted to. Instead she said, "It was nice of you to drive up for Dad's funeral. I'm not sure I thanked you for that."

He looked past her into the apartment. "If I'd been with her, maybe things would be different."

Christy wondered how his presence would have changed

anything. "She died instantly, the police say."

He nodded grimly. "When are you going home to Fairfield?"

"Actually, Neen and Mr. Marle asked me to stay on a while." She gave a little shrug. "I'm supposed to take Cassie's place."

"That's cool." Seamus thought an odd note in Spellman's voice belied his words, as if he'd rather Christy left Toronto, or at least The Vic. Was she a reminder of the woman he'd wronged?

Seamus thought of jumping to Spellman, but Christie had moved away, collecting her purse from the kitchen and her coat from the hall closet.

Henry took the jacket from the chair and began rummaging through the coat's pockets. "I don't suppose you found a cigarette lighter."

"Um, no."

"I don't smoke, but I do carry a lighter," he explained. "I think it was in this coat. Do you think maybe it slipped out somewhere?"

They both bent down to survey the floor near the chair. When they found nothing, Christy looked through the rooms, checking the end table and under the couch cushions. Finally she went to the hall closet and checked the floor there. "I don't see it."

Henry had remained by the door. "Maybe it's in my car."

"I can look for it tonight when I get back here."

After Henry left, Christy stayed a few minutes, being the kind of person who couldn't let something like that go. She made a thorough search of the apartment. No lighter. *At least*, she thought, *I can assure Henry that his lighter isn't at Cassie's place.*

My place, Seamus heard her correct herself as she pulled her slightly sticky front door closed with a firm clunk.

Seamus noticed something as she passed the desk. The crumpled yellow paper, the work order he'd seen earlier, was gone. It was possible Christy had tossed it when he wasn't around, but if she hadn't, then Spellman had picked it up when he gathered his things. It was natural, Seamus told himself, for Spellman to take the receipt, since it was for repairs on his car. But he hadn't mentioned it, which was odd.

Christy started for the subway, and in minutes Seamus heard her wish she'd brought boots to Toronto. Gray, weighty clouds hung like dirty rags overhead, and wet snow fell, making the streets slick and slushy. Women on the street were dressed more for weather than fashion, pairing high-end dress coats with decidedly utilitarian boots with warm linings and non-skid soles. In contrast, Christy tried to pick her way around the wet spots, succeeding only minimally.

Apparently the biggest difference between the twins was their foot size. Cassie had often mentioned that she'd gotten their mother's girl-sized feet while Christy was stuck with their dad's. There was no way Christy could wear her sister's size six boots. In an attempt to keep her suitcase light, she'd brought only the shoes she had on. Now, as they both felt the cold and wet seep into Christy's cute little flats, Seamus heard her promise herself, *When I go home next time, I'll get my Sorels.*

No more than three steps later, she slipped and fell. Seamus was as surprised as Christy when she went down on the dirty sidewalk. It was like being pulled to the ground by a companion's misstep. Her reaction, after a tiny yelp, was to hope no one had seen her ungraceful descent. That was not to be.

"Are you okay, Miss Parker?"

Through Christy's eyes Seamus saw Josh, the young actor from The Vic, standing over her and extending a hand. Taking it, she got back to her feet, undamaged, though Seamus thought she'd have a bruise on the hip where she'd landed. Josh used his scarf to wipe some of the dirty slush off her clothes.

"Thanks," she said as the cold oozed through her wet jeans. "I'm not usually such a klutz."

"Winter in Ontario: who needs it?" he said with a grin.

"Do you live near here?"

"Uh, no." Josh's eyes jerked from right to left and back. "I'm just out walking."

Most people made sojourns outside as brief as possible in this kind of weather. Either Josh was a real snow lover, which Seamus doubted, or he was fibbing about his reasons for taking a morning walk on a frigid day in a neighborhood that was not his.

Busy wiping herself off, Christy was uninterested in the reasons for his presence. Thanking Josh for the rescue she hurried on, vowing as she went that she'd get her boots from Fairfield soon.

Donna was already at work, her girlish figure clad in leggings and a long, belted tunic. "Neen took last night's receipts to the bank. He asked me to get you started."

She led the way up the stairs to the back loft. The staircase, near the back entrance, was in two flights. The first climbed halfway to the loft before turning back on itself at a landing and ascending the rest of the way, ending close to the building's outer wall. The stairs were open, so Christy, and therefore Seamus, could survey the area below them as they went, first the backstage stacked with sets and then, as they traveled the second flight, the auditorium and the stage itself, visible over the heavy black cyclorama.

Crowded against the wall on the left were banks of lights, speakers, and similar electronic enhancements for modern theatres: equipment to provide a range of sounds, lights for special effects, and even pyrotechnics when appropriate. Seamus was interested in how it worked and what it did, but Christy passed without a second glance.

Donna led her down the walkway to the workroom. Along the side opposite the stage, rows of racks filled with neatly hung clothes were open to view, though Seamus noted black curtains that could be drawn to hide the loft from the audience.

Between the rows, along the back wall of the building, shelves contained hatboxes, crates, and bags, all with square labels he couldn't read from that distance. Christy, however, knew they said things like "Gloves, black," and "Pearl necklaces." While Seamus was only mildly interested in the costumes and their accessories, she fairly itched to explore the loft where she was now in charge, or would be once she'd proved herself. She was so excited that she forgot to worry about her ability to handle the job, at least for the moment.

They passed row after row of finished costumes. Bits of glittery fabric and feathers offered tantalizing hints at glamour. More ornate costumes hung with looming dignity near the ends, where support was strongest. Here Christy would have stopped to explore, and Seamus heard her promise herself a good, long look as soon as possible.

When they came to the workroom, Donna unlocked the door with a key from a ring of several. As the door swung open, she handed the ring to Christy. "These were Cassie's." She pointed out specific keys. "This door, the back entrance, the storage rooms. I guess that's your official badge of employment." She made a comic salaam of welcome. "The cast will be in at noon for rehearsals; until then you've got the place to yourself."

"Do you rehearse every day?"

Donna shrugged. "We try. Some of them are students and some have other jobs, because we can't pay them enough to make a living. We have to work around their schedules, which is a pain."

They entered a large room with creaky wooden floors and a low ceiling of cheap acoustical tile. One whole section of wall was corkboard, almost completely covered with designs for *Definitely Dickens* pinned up with everything from ancient thumbtacks to decorative push-pins from various advertisers. Christy was slightly familiar with the sketches from conversations with her twin, but she looked carefully at each one now that she was responsible for turning them into actual costumes. Seamus soon wished she found them less fascinating.

"It's a big job," Donna said, following as she examined the wall.

"Yes," Christy murmured, leaning close to see the detail on a particular drawing. She was more decisive than before, her focus less on *if* she could do this and more on *how* she would get it done. "I suppose you've fitted some of the actors with what you already have."

"Yes," Donna said, "but this is a musical, and some costumes need more glitz than normal Victorian." She pointed out a sketch. "Cassie's plan was that each big number's costumes would follow a theme. This one's all pink and black, with more pink for the girls and more black for the boys."

Christy leaned in to examine the drawing more carefully. "We might have to make some changes, if that's all right. Simplify a little."

Donna shrugged. "Take that up with Neen and Albert." Pointing to a drawing, she said, "I can put together my costume for Little Nell, if that helps. No sequins required."

"Could I get a script?" Christy asked. "It will help me visualize what we're going for."

"I'll get you one right now. Look the place over, and I'll answer your questions when I get back, if I can." Seamus heard her retreating footsteps, first on the wooden floor and then on the metal stairs. He reflected, too late, that he should have gone with Donna. A day with chiffon and satin ranked somewhere near dental surgery on his list of ways he'd like to spend an afternoon.

CHRISTY TOOK A TURN AROUND THE ROOM, examining her new domain. She'd been feeling a little sick off and on, like she'd eaten something that disagreed with her, but she figured that was due to stress. How could she have imagined the changes her life had taken in the last few days? Anyone would be a little queasy.

She continued her tour. There was a computer desk in one corner with the usual assortment of devices: printer, monitor, and brain. Noticing the monitor had been left on, she leaned forward to turn it off. As she did so, she saw a note under the keyboard: "Buy yogurt 4 Chris." The words were scribbled over as if they no longer mattered, something checked off a to-do list by a person unaware it was one of the last things she would accomplish on earth. She had to push the tears away, forcing herself to keep memories of Cassie for when she was alone.

Beyond the desk were two tables, each with a sewing machine threaded and ready. The smaller one had been

Cassie's own machine, the one she preferred to use when possible. The other was an industrial model, capable of sewing heavy fabrics but not as user friendly. Christy looked it over. Mostly it was a more elaborate version of the machines she was used to. Spotting the manual on a shelf overhead, she set it near her purse. Something else to study at home tonight.

The next wall was partitioned into boxes three feet deep that contained bolts of fabric: gauzy greens, spangled reds, and velvety blacks. Christy fingered a few of them, judging the pros and cons of each. Some fabrics were slippery and hard to keep in place as one sewed. Others were so heavy that it was a chore to push them under the needle. None of this kept her from wanting to get to work.

She loved the thrill of starting that first cut, of making a length of fabric into something more by snipping bits of it away. She hadn't sewed for the last few months as her father's illness and death had taken more and more of her time, but before that she'd made everything from Halloween costumes to wedding dresses for the people back home. Although the work she would do here was on a larger scale than she'd attempted before, her fingers itched to get started, to assemble complete outfits from bits and pieces.

There were two large cutting tables in the center of the room. Laid out on one was the costume Cassie had been working on, an all-encompassing robe for the Ghost of Christmas Present. Hanging on a rack nearby were completed outfits for Christmas Past and Christmas Future. She guessed they'd been used before, and Cassie had added shine and sparkle.

A small table to one side held a notebook, and she opened it to find page after page of her sister's handwriting. "A=Magwich/D=Pip." Such notations she easily understood. Albert Marle would play Magwich, the escaped convict from *Great Expectations*, and someone whose name started with "D" would play Pip, the boy he frightened half to death. Donna? She supposed it was an advantage to have someone in the company who could play a child, though she guessed it was no thrill for Donna to be always cast in such roles. She put the notebook on top of the manual for the sewing machine, figuring she should start deciphering her sister's notes as soon as possible.

A noise caught her attention, and she turned, expecting to see Donna. There was no one in the doorway, but a rustling indicated someone was nearby. She stepped out of the workroom, but there was no one there. Hurried footsteps sounded on the metal staircase, and curiosity drew her to the railing.

Christy leaned over the rail and peered down at the dark stage. Nothing moved. Someone had been up here when she and Donna arrived, someone who had hidden until he could exit unseen. Why?

She returned to the workroom. The wall separating it from the costume racks was nothing but pegboard, which was why she'd heard the intruder's movements so clearly. He must have been concealed among the costumes when she and Donna passed. She doubted a prowler would operate at ten in the morning, but if he was a member of the company, why not just introduce himself? In the end she decided someone at The Vic was curious about the new wardrobe mistress but unwilling to be caught spying on her.

Donna returned, apologizing for taking so long. "Neen got held up in the city, and he has the keys to the office. I had to break in to get your script."

"You broke in?"

She shrugged. "This place is so old there isn't any place

you can't get into if you know how. Most of the interior entries have transoms." She pointed to one over the door to the workroom. "I guess they were for light and ventilation. Anyway, if you aren't old and feeble, you can just climb through and get into a room, which is what I did to get you this." Handing Christy the script, she said, "I see you found Cassie's notebook. That will help a lot, because she wrote absolutely everything down."

"She always did." Christy set the book down on the worktable, and the two of them went through it together.

"I'm Pip," Donna said. "I play the children's parts whenever possible, because it's a pain to get real kids. Too many rules and too many interfering parents. It's a challenge for me to make each role different, so it helps if the costumes change my shape as much as possible."

"I'll keep that in mind." She looked at the list. "I take it you're Oliver Twist as well."

Donna gave an impish bow. "At your service. May I please have some more?"

"Okay. 'H' is cast as David Copperfield. Would that be Henry Spellman?"

Her brow descended in disapproval. "You've met him?"

"He came by the apartment this morning."

"Humph! He's a fast worker, that one."

"I know he and Cass were close."

"*Were* is the operative word." Donna raised an eyebrow but apparently decided to change the subject rather than elaborate. "Now, here's what Cassie had in mind for *The Old Curiosity Shop*."

CASSIE SPENT SEVERAL HOURS in her room, angry with everyone, even Ruth, for making her feel confused and doubtful. To reassure herself that she was alive, she made detailed notes about the costumes for *Definitely Dickens,* the next play scheduled at The Vic. She listed what they needed to get for each costume, satisfying herself after several hours' work that she'd covered everything. The only disturbing part was she couldn't remember the names of some of the actors. She listed them by their characters instead, but it was odd that names of people she knew so well wouldn't come to mind.

As she worked, the anger faded and another emotion took its place. She no longer felt the urge to throw things.

She stopped asking herself the same questions over and over, because there were no answers that comforted her. In the end, Cassie found herself wanting nothing more than comfort.

Just before noon, Ruth knocked on the door. "Want to come to lunch with me?"

Cassie overcame the lethargy that had seized her. "Okay." Her mind added, *What can it hurt?*

At the café, she filled a tray, no longer concerned about someone tampering with the food. Maybe if she cooperated, they'd let her go home for a while. They'd see she wasn't a troublemaker, and they'd grant her that much.

From the amazing variety of things offered, she chose coleslaw and a club sandwich speared with decorative toothpicks. When asked what she'd like to drink, she chose Coke. Ruth followed her, centering a tiny salad on her own tray and then surrounding it with a brownie covered with whipped cream, a piece of four-layer walnut cake, a slice of pumpkin pie, a gingerbread cookie, and a dish of French vanilla ice cream.

"Nancy doesn't get it," Cassie complained when they were seated and the utensils had been unwrapped and the trays cleared away. "Can you tell her I really need to get back to Toronto?"

Ruth's eyes rolled upward briefly before she caught herself. "You need to consider the possibility that your life really is over, Cassie."

"That's fine for you to say. You're—well, you're older. You did what you wanted to do, raised your kids and worked with your greyhounds. I haven't finished a third of what I had planned." She dropped the first toothpick beside her plate and picked up half of the sandwich. "Maybe I should explain to her that I'm under contract to The Vic."

"You can't bargain your way out of death." Ignoring the salad, Ruth started with the pie, dumping her scoop of ice cream on top of it. "Darn, I forgot to get a spoon."

"Here. I don't need mine." Cassie tried the coleslaw, which was sweet, just the way she liked it. Did they know this stuff about everybody, or did her "approximated" body adjust what it was given to her likes? She pulled the top piece of bread off her sandwich and examined the items beneath. Under the ham was a layer of pickle, exactly the way her mother used to make it for her when she was a kid, thinly sliced and crisscrossed on top of the cheese. Nobody but Christy knew Cassie liked her club sandwich that way. Nobody living.

With a start, Cassie realized she believed it. It was all true.

Chapter Nine

CHRISTY BEGAN HER CAREER as wardrobe mistress by finishing a costume Cassie had left on the sewing table, and Seamus was bored to tears by mid-afternoon. He sensed but did not understand the elation she felt as seams came together under her hands, as she pressed them flat with a carefully adjusted iron: hot for some fabrics, just beyond warm for others. For hours he waited as she snipped threads and searched drawers under the sewing table for things he'd never heard of, like bias tape and bobbin reels. He felt the fabric slide under her fingers as she guided it to what he learned was a presser foot, but the sensation meant nothing to him. He got no satisfaction from the straight line and un-puckered expanse of a seam after she expertly twisted the threads and cut them with a small blade built into the machine. Her thoughts were totally focused on her work.

Seamus distracted himself with thoughts of what he'd do when he returned to the ship. Mike might have run into someone interested in becoming a cross-back. Nancy, being a counselor, would know who among the recently dead was having trouble leaving life behind permanently. He would tell them what he was looking for, and they could keep an eye out. Since they'd asked him to mentor once before, he was pretty sure they'd be willing to help him find someone suitable.

As Christy sewed, Seamus went over the qualities he'd require until he had a concise but essential list. Brains, curiosity, and something for which there was no precise term: good judgment was as close as he could come. To know when to speak and when to be quiet; when to jump and when to stay; when to step in and when to butt out. That was what made a good cross-back. They'd be more efficient together, covering more territory. They'd share thoughts and theories when their hosts were asleep. They'd be a team, and he wouldn't always be alone. He liked the idea a lot.

It bothered him a little that he was so anxious to have a partner after all this time, but Seamus told himself that people change, even dead people.

Still Christy sewed on, her bottom lip often caught

between her teeth as she concentrated. When a young man he recognized came to ask if she wanted to order out for lunch, Seamus gladly escaped the world of fabric and left with him.

Randy thought of himself as a dancer, but he was also part-time stage hand, player of small roles, and college student with a yen to make it in the theatre. He and Josh were an item, and they headed to a picnic table outside the back door in order to smoke as they ate their lunches. It was cold outside but not unbearable. The snow had stopped, and bright sun lit the tiny patch littered with cigarette butts and sandwich wrappers. The table and its attached benches were draped with a tarp that kept it dry when it wasn't in use. The two folded the cover and hung it over a nearby fence before setting out their lunches and seating themselves on the benches.

Most of their conversation was uninteresting to Seamus, and he wasn't thrilled with Randy's choice of tuna for lunch. It was a taste he'd never been able to like. Feeling the kick of nicotine as the young man lit up, however, Seamus reflected that thorns are often accompanied by roses. With a glance at the door to assure they were alone, Randy voiced what had been bothering him, since Neen had spoken to them the night before. "Everyone thinks we left that stupid guillotine loose."

"They can think what they like," Josh said. "We put it away like always. If it fell, it's because somebody was screwing with it afterwards."

"I know." Randy couldn't let go of what other people thought. "It bugs me, though."

"You saw me do that thing I always do: that nudge to make sure it doesn't wiggle."

"I did. And I checked that the chains were in place, like I always do."

Josh bunched his sandwich wrapper and tossed it into a nearby trash can. "I say somebody screwed with it. Not that they meant to hurt Cassie, but—" He stopped, unable to say why anyone would have tinkered with the piece. "We did our job."

It bothered Seamus that the two men were so certain they'd anchored the guillotine set piece correctly, contradicting what both the inspector and Neen thought. Seamus jumped briefly to Josh, searching his mind for any feeling of guilt or any idea that he was hiding something.

No, Josh was as certain as Randy was that the guillotine had been secure when they left the theatre that night. If that was true, someone had tampered with the set piece, for a reason yet unknown. Could that reason have been to hurt Cassie Parker?

The rest of the conversation was either in a foreign language or beyond Seamus' understanding. It covered topics like "pliés," "fan kicks," and "jazz squares," and was almost as incomprehensible as Christy's sewing terms. Seamus began to look forward to jumping to someone else.

The opportunity came in the person of a young woman in full Victorian regalia whose name he didn't remember. He did, however, recall a sense of mild dislike.

"Hey, guys."

"Hi, Amy," Josh and Randy said in not particularly enthusiastic chorus.

She lit a cigarette and leaned against the doorframe, apparently trying for a glamorous image. It didn't quite work because her bustle got in the way. With a cape over her shoulders as protection from the cold, she created an incongruous combination: proper Victorian lady and self-consciously sexy smoker. Seamus wondered if she thought

Josh and Randy noticed or cared.

As she smoked, Amy wandered the area, wrinkling her nose at the smell when she passed the trash bin. As she neared Randy, Seamus jumped to her. She immediately put a hand to her stomach. "Neen made us do that Nickelby number about thirty times, and I'm feeling kinda sick."

"I felt funny earlier," Randy said. "But I'm better now. Must be the fresh air." He examined the sky above them, almost obscured by the buildings surrounding the theatre.

"If you're sick, don't breathe on me," Josh cautioned. "Marle has been giving me The Look since I missed rehearsal twice last week."

Seamus was quickly finding that Amy didn't have a lot going on in her head. Her thoughts centered on herself: the impression she was making, the impression she might make later, the impression she'd made earlier. At least her thoughts were consistent.

"Did you meet the new costume lady?" Randy asked after the silence stretched too long.

"No. Is she as bitchy as her sister?"

Josh rolled his eyes. "Cassie wasn't hard to get along with, Amy. You just irritated her 'cause you lose a piece off every single costume before you ever get to the stage."

"I only lost a couple things, but she made out like it was some national disaster." After a moment she added, "Kim didn't like her either, so I'm not the only one."

"Kim doesn't like anybody," Josh said with a sniff.

"That's not quite correct, Josh." Randy's smile was innocent. "Kim likes Henry."

"True," Josh agreed. "Could be why she disliked Cassie."

Amy dropped her cigarette, stubbed it out with the toe of her shoe, and kicked the butt from the sidewalk into the snow. "Henry's a grown man. He can date whoever he wants."

With a meaningful glance at Randy, Josh asked, "How'd she steal him from Cassie, anyway?"

Raising one brow, Randy said, "She always brags about winning medals for pistol shooting. Maybe she got the drop on him." He launched into a brief rendition of "You Can't Get a Man with a Gun," and Josh added harmony.

Amy gave them a disgusted look. "I wouldn't expect you two to understand the attraction between a man and a woman."

"Then she *did* use a gun!" Josh whacked Randy's

shoulder, and they burst into laughter.

Amy's nose went up a couple of inches. "Well, I bet the new girl isn't going to be around long."

"Why not?" Randy asked. "She's upstairs right now, sewing her little heart out."

"Kim says she doesn't know a thing about costumes. She's a hick from a hick town."

"Cassie was a hick from that same town, and she was great."

"But Cassie went to school for it," Amy shot back. "This girl doesn't know anything. It'll be a disaster, and Kim says Neen's going to be sorry."

Josh stubbed out his cigarette and rose to go inside. "Kim's always predicting disaster, and you're always spreading her dire forecasts. Why don't you give the woman a chance?"

Amy couldn't think of a reason why she shouldn't, but she wasn't about to admit it. With a lame, "You'll see!" she went back inside, slamming the door in their faces to punctuate her irritation.

CHRISTY WAS AT WORK ON A SLEEVE when she felt a presence beside her. Turning, she saw Albert Marle watching, his expression unreadable.

"Mr. Marle. Hello."

"Good afternoon, Miss Parker. You seem to be settling in well."

She looked down at the jacket, complete except for trim. "So far I'm just putting together what my sister had already cut out. It's not difficult."

He looked at her as if judging something. "Your sister was an excellent seamstress. However, I found her somewhat...fierce, one might say. All business."

Unsure what that meant, Christy rushed to Cassie's defense. "She was a little impatient, I guess, but she was very kind-hearted." A lump formed in her throat at the thought of her sister's absence from the rest of her life. "Cassie was always doing things for people at home, sewing, helping at the library—"

Marle put a warm hand on her shoulder. "I didn't mean to insult her, or you, for that matter. I meant that you seem less likely to judge a person for his foibles."

Her mother had said almost the same thing once. Christy

had been the shy twin, the one who hung back while Cassie got things done and said what she thought. When she groused about it once, wishing aloud that she had Cassie's confidence, her mother had said, "Chris, a person's strengths are her weaknesses, and vice versa. Cassie is sure of herself, but that sometimes makes her intolerant of the opinions of others. You're willing to give people the benefit of the doubt. That isn't a bad thing."

"I'm wondering," Marle said now, his eyes holding Christy's as she imagined a hypnotist might, "if you'd come to my dressing room tomorrow after the show. I have something I'd like to show you."

Before she could reply, there was tittering at the doorway, and she turned to see Kim and Amy hovering just inside the room. Kim whispered something to Amy in a way that left Christy in no doubt that she was the subject of the remark. Amy said a little too loudly, "Donna sent us for fittings."

Marle bowed slightly. "I'll leave you to your work. Please don't forget what I asked."

"I won't." She didn't know if she meant "I won't forget," or "I won't come."

As the director left, the two actresses came a few steps into the room and then stopped, their manner suggesting reluctance.

"Come on over," Christy invited, setting the notebook on the table. "I'll find the pages where all your secrets are written down." It was supposed to be a joke, but neither woman even smiled.

Finally Amy came forward, glancing at her companion as if seeking her indulgence for cooperating with the alien among them. With a pained expression, Kim joined her.

"You're Kim, aren't you?" Christy said. "I enjoyed your Miss Pross last night."

"Maybe you should let the *Star* know you approve," Kim said, widening her eyes and making her voice breathy. "It's hard to get a fresh perspective these days, but I bet Fairfax is as fresh as it gets."

"Fairfield." Christy felt a flush creep up her neck. These women disliked her for no reason she could discern. As they made eye contact, Amy tacitly approving Kim's jab, Christy thought of junior high. She was dealing with Mean Girls without knowing why they were so hostile.

She stuck to business. "I haven't read the whole play yet,

but I wanted to meet everyone and get an idea of who's playing whom."

Kim raised a scornful eyebrow. "When you've read it, you'll see the job's too big for an amateur."

Christy pressed her lips together for a moment, deciding how best to handle the situation. After a moment she picked up the notebook and began turning pages. "Oh," she said, stopping. "Here's a note that says there's special-order fabric coming for Kim's costume. I guess we'll have to wait on that." She gave Kim a polite smile. "If you don't mind, I'll let you go and work with Amy for a few minutes."

Kim looked surprised, then doubtful. "Special order?"

"Yes." Christy closed the book with a snap before the two women could see the note, which was nonexistent. "It seems Cassie had something unique in mind for you."

There was not much Kim could do except leave, and she did, her expression betraying confusion and foreboding. Had Cassie and Kim been such enemies that Kim dreaded the "unique" costume Cassie might have planned for her?

Christy was pleased with herself. She'd initiated a divide and conquer ploy, choosing Amy as the person more easily won over. Once Kim was gone, Christy chatted in a friendly way, describing her idea to help Amy with the difficult costume change she was experiencing. "That would be great." Amy's expression lost some of its earlier coldness. "Neen's always after me about it."

"Good. Now let's see what you'll be doing in the new show."

As they paged through the notebook again, Amy explained that a musical offered her a featured role, since she was primarily a dancer. "I'm Estella from *Great Expectations*," she said, leaning over to point at the drawing Cassie had done. "She's very pretty but kind of a snob."

"I've read the book," Christy said lightly. "This drawing is nice, but let me show you what I have in mind for her." Finding a blank page, she quickly sketched a lithe figure in a diaphanous gown of white with a ballerina-style skirt, puffy sleeves, and a tiara of flowing ribbons. If Christy's assessment of Amy was correct, she could make her into an ally with a beautiful costume.

When she finished, Amy's face lit with delight. "That's gorgeous!" Suddenly she was downright chatty, explaining the intricacies of her dance and sharing her thoughts about how the skirt would drape as she moved. Ten minutes later, as Christy watched her go, she figured Amy might still be reserved when Kim was around, but she was no longer Christy's enemy.

ALL AFTERNOON SEAMUS WORKED HIS WAY through the company, picking up gossip from cast and crew as he went. Nothing suggested evil on the part of any individual, though there were the usual likes and dislikes among them. Marle was considered eccentric, but that was not unusual for the profession. Neen was well-liked, and his wife Donna was too, except for a few who'd faced the sharp edge of her tongue when they made fun of their director. No one Seamus found felt animosity toward Cassie, and most of them seemed genuinely shocked and saddened by her death.

He jumped to Josh just after he completed a difficult dance segment. As the young man recovered his breath in the wing, Seamus learned he was avoiding Marle because he'd missed several rehearsals. His reasons remained in the back of his mind where Seamus couldn't reach them, but he sensed more embarrassment than evil intent.

Unfortunately, Josh soon returned to rehearsing, which meant that Seamus participated in several dance numbers. After he'd been jarred by tap and made nauseous by jazz turns, he jumped to someone else. Big mistake. With his new host, he learned how terrifying ballet can be. And if he'd ever wondered what went through the mind of a ballerina *en pointe*, the answer was "Ow! Ow! Ow!"

He looked for an opportunity to move to someone who wasn't a dancer. It was convenient for him, then, though not for Josh, when Albert Marle stood waiting in the wings when the dancers took a break. Seamus jumped to Marle as his current host passed. The director pulled Josh aside to ask some pointed questions about his recent absences. "It won't happen again," Josh insisted, raising both hands as if warding off a blow. "I had some kind of bug. I thought I was over it then it hit me again."

Marle released Josh with a stern reminder that they were a company and every person's presence at rehearsal was important.

"I know." Josh's tone hinted he'd say anything to get away. "I'll be here from now on."

The company was off duty between rehearsals and the

evening show. Seamus had a nice dinner of steak and asparagus with Albert Marle in his top-floor apartment at the front of the building. Marle's mind revealed no guilt; he seemed a man perfectly at ease with himself, though Seamus suspected there was something odd about Marle. Did he dislike the man? The feeling wasn't that strong. It was more discomfort than dislike.

Still, Marle was a professional who wanted his theatrical presentations to come off well. His mind fluttered over a mental to-do list that he attacked methodically when he returned to the stage to prepare for the evening show. Marle spoke to everyone he met and tried to make each person feel important to the whole effort. When the curtain rose, he immersed himself in his role wholeheartedly, becoming for the duration of the play Jarvis Lorry, banker and friend to the Manettes.

CHRISTY WORKED LIKE THE PROVERBIAL DOG ALL DAY. With Donna's help, she completed several costumes, at least in terms of being ready to fit to the actors who'd wear them. She'd add trims and detail as time permitted, and a few in the troupe were willing to help with that. She met almost everyone in the company: the gruff stage hands, the stage and lighting techs who seemed to speak a foreign language, the set designer who dressed and even spoke in a charming, antique, Fred Astaire style, and a variety of actors from youthfully confident beginners to tiring but productive old hands.

When performance time approached, she went downstairs to do a costume check, humming a number from the upcoming show she'd heard over and over all day. Neen had given her the names of a few actors who needed to be watched. Amy, dubbed "Amy the Airhead" by Donna, often left important parts of her costume behind when she went onstage. In addition, a couple of the students earning college credit by playing small roles had been known to cheat for their own comfort. One had once worn flip-flops under her floor-length gown, claiming the high-button boots she'd been given hurt her feet, and one of the boys tended to leave his necktie off because it choked him.

"They don't get that it pulls the audience out of the story when they spot something like that," Neen said with a disgusted grimace. "It'll help if you keep an eye on them."

Everyone was properly costumed tonight, and aside from a few minor episodes, Christy's help was unnecessary. She watched from her corner, still feeling lucky to be part of the show. During intermission, she returned the prop table to order. She didn't intend to eavesdrop, but two actresses on the other side of the London street set didn't know she was there.

"She seems to know what she's doing," one said. Christy didn't know the cast well enough to name them by voice, but she thought it was the woman who played the determinedly prayerful Mrs. Cruncher.

The second voice had reservation in its tone. "It's not hard to take over a show that's already costumed and keep it going. We'll know more with the next show."

"That'll be a job," the first woman agreed. "After that it gets even harder, because she'll have to design the costumes herself."

"Poor Cassie!" the other said. "We'll miss her."

"Yeah. I wonder how that jerk Henry feels now."

"Oh, Henry's just weak," the second woman claimed. "Kim's been after him forever, and she finally got him while Cassie was away."

"When a guy cheats on his girlfriend, it's his fault, not hers," the other said firmly. "No matter how much Kim came on to him, Henry should have thought about Cassie."

A third voice interrupted, and the subject turned to the second half of the performance. Christy moved quietly away, unwilling to be seen by the women who'd discussed her and her sister. She felt pity for Cassie and anger at Henry Spellman. The woman who'd blamed him was correct in Christy's view: a man who'd been sleeping over at his girlfriend's was obliged to resist a come-on from a weasel like Kim Snyder.

As Christy was leaving the theatre after the performance, a hand on her shoulder stopped her, and she turned to see Tarcie Starpon, the delicate blond who played Lucy Manette. "I wonder if we might have a word." It sounded like an order, not a request.

"Of course." Christy stepped aside to allow several others to exit. She followed Tarcie to a spot backstage, where the actress turned and examined her languidly. "You're Cassie's little sister."

"Twin sister." Although Neen had asked all the actors to visit the wardrobe room and introduce themselves to help

Christy get acclimated, Tarcie had not yet made the trip. From her manner, Christy got the impression the new costumer was far down Tarcie's list of important people.

Glancing around to assure they were alone, Tarcie said, "I hear you're invited to Albert's apartment tomorrow night." Her lips were tight with disapproval.

Christy wondered how she'd found out. Amy or Kim, probably. Was the whole company laughing about the new girl's dilemma? And why did Tarcie Starpon care? She paused, unsure how to answer.

Tarcie leaned toward her, and Christy was overcome with strong perfume. She forced herself not to step back as the actress asked, "Do you intend to go?"

Christy took a deep breath. "I'm not sure why you're asking, Miss Starpon."

Tarcie's tone turned even more disapproving. "Mr. Marle is your employer, Miss Parker. It's not appropriate for you to—"

To her own surprise, Christy heard herself interrupting. "Mr. Marle is an adult, and so am I. Between us, we're able to decide what's appropriate. Now if you'll excuse me." With shaking legs, Christy stepped around the speechless actress and made her escape.

Chapter Ten

CHRISTY AVOIDED ALBERT MARLE THE NEXT DAY, keeping busy in the back loft where she now presided. It was comfortable for her, since Cassie had organized things in much the same way she would have. The room bore a faint resemblance to their sewing room at home, but on a larger scale. Fabric was stored in plain view so she could see at a glance what was available and how much of it there was. Thread and other sewing notions were kept in clearly labeled drawers. Worktables were clear except for projects underway.

As she folded the pieces of the dress she was making for Amy's dance number, movement caught her attention. She looked up to see Kim in the doorway, looking like she was about to jump into a pit of snakes. "I snagged the zipper in this dress. It might need to be replaced."

"Let me see." Approaching, Christy turned Kim around and examined the zipper, which was well and truly stuck. "Can you wiggle out of it and leave it here?"

"Neen wants us to practice in costume," she said. "We have to learn how to step over all these skirts."

Christy sighed. "Okay, I'll see what I can do, but you still have to take it off."

Kim frowned. "I can't stand around here practically naked." Her tone implied Christy was stupid not to have thought of it. Christy was reminded that she had to come up with a "unique" costume for Kim, as she'd mentioned. *See?* She told herself. *Lies make trouble, no matter how clever your intentions might be.*

Pointing to the changing room, she ordered, "Go in there and toss it out to me."

Rolling her eyes only a little, Kim did as directed. Christy went to work on the zipper.

"Excuse me. I'm looking for Kim Snyder." The man who entered the room rather hesitantly was tall, with short brown hair, high cheekbones, and brown eyes that narrowed when they met Christy's.

"She's in there," Christy said, indicating the closed door. "I'm fixing her dress."

"Oh." He seemed unsure where that left him. "If you don't mind, I'll wait. I stopped in last Thursday, but the place was all closed up. Some emergency, I guess."

"Yes." She went back to work on the zipper, carefully pulling fabric from the metal teeth. "This won't take long. The damage isn't as bad as I first thought."

"No hurry."

As Christy worked, the man wandered around the room. He seemed vaguely familiar, and he glanced at her from time to time as if wanting to say something. "You make all these costumes?" he finally asked.

"I'm new here," she responded, "but I'll be in charge of making them from now on."

He fingered the fabric of Christmas Past's costume. "Hectic but fun, I suppose."

"Exactly."

"So if you play for a living," he said, stressing the word *play* to highlight the pun, "what do you do in your free time?"

"I haven't been in Toronto long," Christy responded, pronouncing the city's name as residents did, "Trono." She'd reached the tricky part, where she might easily tear the fabric if she wasn't careful, but she added, "I come from a really small town where there weren't many choices for entertainment if you weren't into mailbox baseball."

He chuckled. "That town—would it be—"

"You didn't tell me we had company." Kim had opened the door to peer out at them.

Christy might have disappeared in a puff of smoke as the man took a step forward and then stopped, apparently intimidated. "Miss Snyder. I was hoping to talk with you for a few minutes."

"I'm in my underwear." Kim threw an irritated glance at Christy.

"I'll find you something to put on." Hurrying out to the costume racks, Christy selected a dressing gown in deep violet. *Perfect for Kim's hair and skin*, she thought almost regretfully. She didn't feel like helping the actress look good for her attractive visitor, but she couldn't leave her huddling in the dressing room in her skivvies. Well, she could, but she wasn't the type.

Of course Kim looked stunning in the robe. After the few seconds it took to put it on and release her dark hair from the casual ponytail she'd been wearing, she emerged like Cleopatra from her barge, regal and glowing.

"Sorry to keep you waiting." She managed to imply with

a glance it was Christy's fault.

Their visitor looked star-struck. "I'm Chief Damen's son, John, Miss Snyder," he said. "I understand he called about your trip to Mason's Bridge last weekend."

Kim lowered her eyes for a moment. "You're here about that terrible accident."

"He asked me to interview you in person." Judging from his slightly goofy expression, Christy thought it was more likely John Damen had begged for the job. He was obviously in awe of Kim, or at least the star he imagined her to be. "You probably know, the chief is pretty thorough."

Kim gave Damen a smile Christy had seen only on stage until now. "Of course I remember. In school, I got more than one thorough lecture about driving too fast."

Christy had returned to work on the zipper, politely pretending she wasn't hearing everything they said. Glancing at her, Kim took Damen's arm. "Let's go out where we can speak privately."

Ironically, she led him to a spot on the other side of the pegboard wall, which meant that though she couldn't see them, Christy heard every word of their conversation.

"Dad probably told you part of it," Damen began.

"Sometime around midnight on February 19th, there was a hit and run on Barley Road. A couple who'd run out of gas was walking home when a car came over a rise at high speed and hit them both."

"Terrible!" Kim made clicks with her tongue. "He said the woman died instantly."

"Yes. The man is in critical condition and hasn't been able to speak yet."

"The person who hit him didn't stop to see if he was alive?"

"No."

"How awful! And you're investigating the incident for your father?"

"I live here in the city, so I offered to help him out." He went on with the explanation, patently trying to impress Kim. "Dad doesn't have much of a budget for travel, but everyone was interested to hear you were in town last weekend for your sister's wedding. And your parents live on Barley Road."

Kim's tone turned cool, more like the Kim Christy knew. "Then I'm a suspect?"

Damen's voice revealed dismay. "Oh, no, Miss Snyder.

We were just hoping you saw something out there.”

Kim sounded slightly mollified by his assurances. “I’m afraid you’ve wasted a trip.”

Damen waved a hand. “It’s okay. I only live about ten miles from here.” His voice turned slightly wistful. “I always admired you in school, and I thought it would be great to meet you in person.”

“That’s sweet!” Kim said. “But I can’t help you. I certainly didn’t hit those people.”

“Of course not.” He sounded horrified at the suggestion. “You don’t even own a car.”

Her tone changed slightly. “That’s right. I don’t.”

“That’s what my dad said.” Christy heard his feet shift on the uneven wood floor. “Well, then, I’ll—” He paused as if remembering. “If you don’t have a car, how did you get to Mason’s Bridge?”

“My boyfriend drove me. But we were never on Barley Road. We stayed at the inn downtown, not at my parents’ house.” She added in an aggrieved tone, “I avoid my mother whenever possible.”

Damen sighed. “We hoped you might have seen the car, but if you stayed in town—”

"We did. And the next morning we left early in order to get here for the matinee."

Christy heard a sigh. "Sorry to have taken up your time, Miss Snyder."

"Please, call me Kim," she said, her voice warm again. "I'll walk down with you and sign a souvenir program. That way your trip isn't completely wasted."

By that time Christy had fixed the zipper. She went to the doorway to hand the dress back to Kim, who took it and headed downstairs with the handsome John Damen without a single word of thanks. Damen looked back once, meeting Christy's gaze, but she turned away, ignoring what might have been a plea for understanding. What did she care if a man she'd never seen before had a massive crush on Kim Snyder?

When Christy came downstairs a few minutes later to fit a costume to its owner, Damen stood in the wings, talking to Henry Spellman. She heard Henry confirm they'd never been on the road where the accident occurred. As she started back upstairs, she heard Damen tell Spellman, "That's exactly what Miss Snyder said."

As the staircase turned, she looked down and caught

Damen's eye on her. He smiled, and Christy nodded in what she hoped was a neutral manner. He seemed interested in her again now that Kim was out of sight. It was irritating, but there was that vague feeling that she knew him from somewhere. Warm brown eyes followed her until she disappeared at the top of the stairs.

A few minutes later, she heard his voice again. "Christy Parker?" She looked up, and Damen entered, wearing a grin she didn't understand. "I asked your name downstairs."

Christy waited, still put off by the fact that his initial friendliness to her had disappeared as soon as Kim turned her artificial charm on him.

"I wanted to talk to you."

"I thought you came to see Miss Snyder." She unconsciously used the awe-struck tone he'd used when speaking to Kim.

"That is what I came here for, but—" Damen took a step into the room. "Do you remember Johnny Canby?"

The name flooded her mind with memories. Johnny Canby had been their friend and neighbor growing up, so frequent a visitor that his appearance in the yard immediately caused her mother to set another plate at the table. Johnny, Christy, and Cassie had for several years seen themselves as three musketeers, all for one and one for all.

The Parker girls had known Johnny's home life wasn't the greatest. His hair was oddly cut, his clothes were second-hand and wrinkled, and he never invited them to the run-down modular in the middle of a field where grass grew sparingly and everything seemed a little cock-eyed. He'd never made a big deal of it. Johnny was simply Johnny.

For his part, Johnny had never questioned that the twins were a package. It didn't seem to bother him that they finished each other's sentences and sounded exactly alike on the phone. He was never fooled by their attempts to switch places, but he played along when others were involved, calmly calling Christy "Cass" when the trick called for it. None of them had the devices for social networking other kids had, Johnny due to finances and the girls due to their father's distrust of technology. As a result, they'd been considered odd at school, but when the three of them stuck together, who cared?

Along with being the only neighbor even close to their age, Johnny was full of fun, always ready to take on their adventures and propose his own. They'd roamed the farm, exploring the pond in spring, the woods in summer, and the barn in fall, when the hay was stacked up almost to the ceiling. In winter, they'd spent time in the musty attic of the Parker home, combing through old picture albums and dreaming of faraway places.

Their comfortable friendship had changed suddenly when they were twelve. One morning Johnny showed up at the door, his expression stony. Looking past him, Christy saw his mother waiting impatiently in the dusty driveway. Their 1986 Plymouth was packed to the roof with blankets, boxes, and suitcases. She was smoking, as usual, and the car was already filled with a blue haze.

"We're moving," Johnny said, his eyes seeking Christy's. At that moment it felt like she'd stepped off the planet.

Only the week before, he'd kissed her in the Parkers' barn. Cassie had gone into the house, and Christy realized later he'd manipulated the situation, asking for something for the first time ever. Slightly surprised when he expressed a wish for a cold drink, Cass nevertheless went willingly enough to get them each a can of soda. As Johnny and Christy sat waiting for her, side by side on a hay bale, he'd leaned over and kissed her on the lips, taking his time about it. She'd been surprised and, in the end, quite pleased.

She hadn't seen Johnny since the day he came to say goodbye, but she'd always remembered the kiss and what he said afterward: "Cass is all right, but I like you best."

"Johnny—" Ten—no, thirteen years later, she didn't know what to say.

"First, I want to ask you to forgive my behavior earlier. Kim wasn't very gracious when my dad called to tell her I was coming to interview her, so I figured I'd play the star-struck hometown boy." He grinned again. "Besides, I wasn't sure you were you."

She was still in shock. "I didn't recognize you."

He waved a hand. "Why would you recognize the ragamuffin you used to be nice to?"

She rose, taking a step toward him. "I never thought of you that way."

"I did." He moved his feet as if shifting gears mentally. "Anyway, Kim responds best to flattery, but I didn't mean to insult you in the process."

"I'm just glad to see you again, Johnny—" She stopped. "I suppose it's John now?"

"Mostly, yes. And I took my stepfather's name, Damen. He's been really good to me."

"I—we always wondered about you." She frowned. "You never wrote or called."

He examined the floor for a moment. "I figured you'd forget all about me. I used to tell myself, 'A girl like her will have boyfriends standing in line.'" His eyes met hers. "Was I right?"

Christy chose her words carefully, wanting to be truthful without letting too much truth slip out. "There were boyfriends, but never another guy like Johnny Canby."

That embarrassed him. Turning away, he examined the costume drawings again. When he spoke, it was as if they'd said all that was necessary about the past. "You're pretty brave to take on the job of costuming a whole play."

She grimaced. "Sometimes I think brave; other times I think crazy."

"Maybe we can go out some time and catch up, you know?"

Christy caught herself thinking how great it would be when she told Cass that she'd found Johnny Canby. But no. There'd be no more of that.

"Yes, we need to catch up on what's happened since eighth grade. I'm busy here evenings, but I can take an hour off for lunch most any day."

"Sounds good." As he backed away and out the door, his smile reminded Christy that she'd never really forgotten Johnny Canby.

CASSIE DIDN'T SLEEP AT ALL THAT NIGHT, not that it mattered. She wasn't real. She wasn't Cassie anymore. She was some sort of illusion, created to fool herself. She might breathe and eat and walk around, but the truth was, she was dead. She'd tried a dozen alternative explanations, up to and including alien abduction. Nothing fit except what she'd been told. She was dead.

That's when the tears fell, first a few and then so many her throat became raw and the muscles in her face spasmed with fatigue. Finally she lay exhausted, trying to think about nothing at all.

She heard light taps on her stateroom door but ignored them. The first occasion came early, around seven. When she didn't answer, whoever it was went away. A second attempt was made at nine. She ignored that one too. What was the point of seeing anyone? What use in talking? If she really was dead, nothing would change it. Nothing could give her back what she most wanted.

At eleven fifty, the knock came again. When she didn't answer, she heard Ruth's voice. "Cassie? I was hoping you'd go to lunch with me."

"Cassie?" Ruth said a few seconds later. "I hate to eat alone."

Cassie lay on the bed, dressed in the clothes she'd worn since arriving, heedless of the fact she hadn't even removed her shoes in deference to the white coverlet. She rolled over to face the wall. No. She didn't want to make nice with anyone, especially anyone as dead as she was.

She reached out for a pillow to cover her head with, but Ruth said, "I have a confession to make. Come to lunch with me, and I'll tell you everything."

Ten minutes later, Ruth slathered mayonnaise on her burger and pressed the bun down, compressing it to a manageable size for biting, and made her confession. It was not what Cassie expected. "I'm a quantum physicist."

Shocked out of her funk, Cassie said, "I thought you were

a rancher who raised greyhounds."

"I'm that too." Ruth speared a fry and dunked it into the wide circle of ketchup she'd squirted on her plate. "I don't tell people how I made my living, because they go all quiet and can't think of anything to say."

Despite her gloomy mood, Cassie made a joke. "Gee, Ruth, I don't know what to say."

Ruth chewed, swallowed, and sipped her root beer. "I'm only telling you now because you need to hear some things about mankind in general and modern mankind in particular."

"Look, Ruth, I'm trying to understand. I really am. It's just hard."

Her friend's expression softened. "I know, darlin', I know. It's one thing for an old biddy like me to kick off, but someone like you—" Ruth must have sensed Cassie was fighting tears, because she abruptly began the story of her own past.

"I lived for eighty-seven years, and until my health failed completely, I spent a lot of time trying to understand the universe. I studied the big things: stars, galaxies, the cosmos, but I also studied the smallest things: atoms, quarks, and mesons."

Now Cassie smiled thinly. "I don't even know what the last two are."

Ruth waved a hand dismissively. "Doesn't matter. My point is that in those years, we discovered new thing after new thing after new thing about existence and life and what is. But every new thing we learned opened up areas bigger than what we'd imagined. Every time, we realized that what we'd learned was just a little bit of what was left to learn." She popped the fry she'd been waving into her mouth and finished with, "I have a feeling that's how it's always been, and how it always will be."

"But science has proved—"

"A lot of things," Ruth interrupted. "But if we're honest, we have to admit we don't know much. We've looked into space, and it's bigger than we can even conceive. We've looked into the atom, and it's pretty much nothing. We don't know how atoms make themselves into inanimate things then into animate things. We certainly don't understand how a living being moves and talks one second and begins to rot away the next. We call it death, but we don't know what that means."

Cassie was fascinated. "But why do so many scientists reject religion?"

Ruth sniffed. "We're arrogant creatures who don't want to admit to ignorance. In every generation, men of learning contend we know almost everything and soon we'll have it all. But really, we don't know much, and without knowing, all we have is faith." She grinned. "Have you ever read Robert Jastrow's comment about a scientist's nightmare?"

Cassie didn't even know who that was but guessed he was a scientist.

Ruth closed her eyes. "He said something like: 'For the scientist who has lived by his faith in the power of reason, the story ends like a bad dream. He has scaled the mountains of ignorance; he is about to conquer the highest peak; as he pulls himself over the final rock, he is greeted by a band of theologians who have been sitting there for centuries.' That might be how it really is, I think."

Cassie tossed her head. "But faith means something different to every person. I read and read to find things I could believe, and in the end, I didn't believe any of it."

Ruth grinned wryly as she speared another fry. "That's your mistake, Darlin'. Whatever made you think what you or I believe has anything at all to do with what *is*?"

Chapter Eleven

ONCE AGAIN SEAMUS WAS DISGUSTED with himself for not jumping when the chance came. He'd stayed with Albert Marle, figuring that if anything was amiss with the running of the theatre, he'd learn about it from the director. But Marle spent the morning away from the Vic, meeting producers, sponsors, promoters, and more. By the time he was finished, Seamus was heartily sick of the business end of things. Who knew there was so much to dressing up and pretending to be someone else? Other than the fact that the place ran on a shoestring, he found nothing suspicious or even very interesting.

When Marle returned to the theatre, it was time for rehearsals for *Definitely Dickens*. Actors milled around, waiting, dressed in casual clothes that allowed free movement and self-expression. Seamus saw Kim and Amy whispering in a corner and felt Albert's flash of irritation as he saw Henry Spellman chatting with an admiring group of dancers. *Jealous,* Seamus figured. The old lion needed the young one, but he didn't have to like him. Spellman was all Marle must once have been and more, since he had the stature of a leading man and didn't need lifts in his shoes and a padded jacket.

"Are we going to start soon, Albert?"

The voice at his elbow caused another stab of irritation. Turning, Marle faced his leading actress. "Soon, Tarcie." Due to his small stature, they were eye to eye, but he avoided her gaze, looking around instead. "Everyone seems to be here."

"Would you like me to get them onstage?"

Seamus heard in his thought something about the softness of her face and the hard-as-nails personality it disguised. Forcing a pleasant tone, he put a hand on Tarcie's arm. "No, thank you, my dear. Neen will be ready shortly."

Tarcie was clearly disappointed she wouldn't be allowed to order the cast around. *She can hardly bear it,* Seamus heard in Marle's head. *So anxious to take my place.*

"Albert," Tarcie's tone might have been playful if there hadn't been reproach in it somewhere. "You weren't, um, doing anything with Cassie Parker, were you?"

Spine stiffening, Marle forced his initial retort back and simply said, "No, Tarcie. She was our wardrobe mistress. That's all."

Tarcie straightened his collar, which was in no need of attention. "And this new one, Christy? I don't mean to pry, honestly. I just don't want—"

She stopped, and Marle finished for her. "You don't want me to make a fool of myself with a young woman in my employ."

"You're not a fool, Albert," Tarcie assured him in a throaty purr. "Just too trusting sometimes." Checking to see that no one was looking, she kissed her index finger and then placed it on his cheek. "I'm only watching out for you, you know."

"I know." But as Tarcie walked away, Marle's thought added, *And for yourself.*

After rehearsal, Seamus jumped to Donna, with whom he was comfortable. Her outlook on the world was pragmatic, but she was not a grumpy person, which was how he liked to see himself. No flowery tributes, no rose-colored glasses, just common sense applied to all situations.

At a break in rehearsals, Donna joined Neen, Albert, and

Tarcie, who was critiquing the progress of the show as if she were in charge. Albert insisted things were moving along well. He seemed to have a schedule in mind as to where they should be at a given point in order to be ready for opening night. When Christy came down the stairs, a costume over each arm, he turned to his lead actress as if one of his to-do items had just come to mind. "I hope you aren't neglecting your fittings, Tarcie. I know Cassie had to practically chase you down to get your cooperation, and I don't want Christine to have more problems than she already has."

Christy must have heard the admonition as she joined the group, and she blushed deeply, probably unhappy to be the cause of Tarcie's chastisement.

Tarcie's eyes flashed angrily toward Christy, but she recovered and put on a smile. "I did my duty some time ago, Albert. Cassie wrote everything down in her book." She turned to Christy. "I bet my Dora costume is well under way by now."

Seamus saw Christy's surprise, as did Donna, who moved to her side like a protective Rottweiler.

Tarcie, too, caught the look. "I hope you haven't lost your sister's notes."

Having watched her page through Cassie's notebook several times, Seamus understood Christy's confusion. He could recall no page devoted to a costume for Dora.

Tarcie's lips twitched in the tiniest of smiles at the chance to pay Christy back for standing up to her earlier. She either had to accuse her sister of mislaying important notes or admit that she had.

"Of course Cassie wrote it down, Miss Starpon, and I've started work on Dora's dress. Now please excuse me. There's Noreen." Moving to where an actress had emerged from the dressing room in a half-finished costume, she began critically examining the fit of the dress, apparently unworried about anything past that.

After a few minutes Donna hurried up the stairs and found Christy in the workroom, pinning up the hem of Noreen's dress. Standing back to judge her work, she said, "All right. Take it off and I'll finish it."

Donna waited until Noreen was gone to ask, "Did Tarcie just put you on the spot?"

"I'm pretty sure she meant to." Christy went to the wall and pointed. "Cassie had drawn a rough sketch of her outfit, but there's nothing about it in the book. I should have noticed it was missing, but there's just so much to think about!" Christy's calm evaporated, and she sounded desperate.

"It would have to be one of the complicated ones," Donna murmured, examining the sketch. To Seamus, the dress looked more like a birthday cake than wearing apparel.

Christy paged through the book as if Cassie's notes might magically appear with one more search. "There are entries on everything except that dress. No size, no measurements, no notes." She sighed. "I wish she'd—I don't know."

"Give you half a chance? Tarcie loves to play mind games." She put a hand on Christy's shoulder. "I'm surprised she went after you already. You just got here."

Christy shrugged, her expression neutral. "I guess we all have to be tested."

"Humph!" Donna glanced around the room. "So what have we got for Dora?"

"Nothing!" Christy looked around in despair. "I've been so busy just keeping up!" She ran both hands through her hair. "My father used to tell me to break things down into manageable parts, and I thought I had, but where do I fit in making another complete costume, and an elaborate one at that?"

"Have you read the scene with Dora?" Donna asked.

"No, and I don't think I ever read *David Copperfield*, though I might have seen the movie as a kid."

Donna gestured at the ruffled Victorian dress Cassie had sketched. "Dora's gorgeous. David falls for her at first sight, marries her, and tries to give her everything she wants. Even when it's obvious she isn't very smart, he still worships her."

"Is that where the term 'Dumb Dora' comes from?" Christy said, a faint grin lighting her features.

"Perfect role for Tarcie." Donna said, returning the grin. "You know what? Cassie kept a master file." She went to a shelf over the desk and selected an anonymous ring binder. "*S, S,*" she muttered, turning the pages quickly until she found the one she wanted. "Here—Tarcie Starpon," she said exultantly. "When an actor became a permanent part of the troupe, Cassie transferred their information to this book so she'd always have a starting point for costuming. These notes are three years old, but if you cut a little on the generous side, it should work." She tilted her head toward the sketch. "The question is can you handle a dress like that, along with all this other stuff?"

"Maybe, if I stay up for the next four nights." Christy grimaced, looking around at the array of costumes in various stages of completion. Seamus knew she'd just begun to be optimistic about getting it all done. Now Tarcie had complicated things. The worst part was, the actress had meant to do exactly that.

CASSIE RETREATED to her stateroom once more to think about what Ruth had said. *Arrogant* was the word she'd used for humankind, and Cassie had to admit, she'd been as arrogant as anyone, declaring there was no life after death simply because she couldn't conceive of it. She found herself talking aloud, trying to get her head around it. "Ruth thinks we're incapable of complete understanding and that something beyond us is in charge. It's Nancy's job to make the whole thing clear. Tomorrow, I'll make her explain everything to me." Turning down the sheets in preparation for her first sleep since arriving, she kicked off her shoes and crawled inside the perfectly comfortable bed.

When the show ended that night, Christy intended to disappear quickly, but events conspired against her. One of the men in the company had torn the sleeve of his shirt half off in a fight scene. Promising to fix it before tomorrow, she hurried upstairs, dropped the shirt on her worktable, and started back down, hoping to slip out and go home. Albert Marle was waiting between her and freedom.

"I hope you haven't forgotten our date, Christine."

"Uh, I'm a little tired," she began.

"This won't take long, and I think you'll find my place quite interesting."

What could she do? Marle was her boss, but he obviously wanted to be more than that. He'd found Cassie intimidating. Was that because she'd refused to visit his little hideaway upstairs?

"Mr. Marle, I don't—"

His expression turned slightly mocking and his eyes glinted with sardonic amusement. "Christine! You're afraid of me!"

"No, it isn't that—" Actually, it was, but she didn't want to seem like the timid country mouse, unsure of the ways of city folk.

Marle put a warm hand on her shoulder. "Let me assure you that I conduct myself as a gentleman at all times."

Is that why they call strip joints "gentlemen's clubs?" she asked herself, though she didn't have the nerve to say it aloud.

"I won't keep you long, but I do want to show you some things."

Come up to my place and I'll show you my etchings. Ordering herself to stop the mental smart remarks, Christy took a deep breath. "Okay. But I really am tired, and I can't stay long." There. She'd provided herself with an excuse to leave if the guy got too friendly. There was the question of how to simplify Cassie's designs for the revue, so maybe he did want to talk about work. She told herself it was ridiculous to think a man like Marle would want to seduce the new wardrobe girl.

As he took her arm in a gallant gesture, she saw Tarcie watching from a few feet away. Her expression promised retribution. Christy turned away, hoping her face didn't reveal her dread of both the next few hours with Albert and the next few days with Tarcie.

The apartment was nice. Marle insisted on drinks, so she chose wine, something she could sip slowly. It got complicated when he gave her a choice, however. Christy had never paid much attention to such things. When she went to dinner at someone's house, if they served wine, she drank it. When Albert named three possibilities, she chose Merlot because she liked the word. It sounded silky.

Once they drinks in hand, Marle turned to her, glass raised. "Here's to tolerance."

"Tolerance." Christy raised her glass and then drank. The wine tasted sour, but she smiled anyway. Holding her glass in one hand, she looked around. Comfortably furnished and perfect for a bachelor who lived for his work, she guessed it was also convenient for entertaining guests. It was a bit of a showplace, more so than most men who lived alone would bother creating. She checked the layout carefully in case she had to get out quickly.

"I've spent thirty years in the theatre," Albert told her, waving at the array of pictures on one wall. Dutifully Christy went there and traced Marle's life in photographs. She squinted at a picture of Marle and a young man with long, frizzy hair standing before a large house on a summer day.

"Recognize that fellow?"

She leaned closer to examine the face. "Is that Henry Spellman?"

Marle chuckled. "It is. When I found him he was working with a group of improvisational actors. They'd rented that house, out in the suburbs near Brampton. They'd intended to become the next Second City, but it wasn't going well. The five of them couldn't seem to get on together, and three had just moved on when I saw Henry's work and realized he had acting talent. He was stuck with a two-year lease on the house they'd rented, so he was grateful for the job I offered." He pointed to the side of the picture, where she could see the corner of a building. "Henry got the job he badly needed, and I got a place to keep my car out of the weather in the bargain. I seldom use it, but one wants an automobile, just the same." He nodded to himself. "I think Henry is happy here, despite the change his career took when he left improv for classic theatre."

"Audiences seem to like him," Christy said, omitting any comment on her own view of Henry. He was a good actor. Maybe that made up for not being a great human being.

She continued down the line of photographs. The earliest

ones showed "Little Albert" dressed for various Shakespearean roles. "My mother was an actress well known at Stratford and in several prestigious touring companies. I first played one of Macduff's murdered brood and then moved on to playing youths like Prince Hal, young Malcolm, and Romeo's cousin Benvolio." Marle came over and stood behind her, closer than she would have liked. "I loved theatre but never took to Shakespeare."

"You've done so much," she said, moving down the line and away from Marle.

"After a mildly distinguished career at various theatres, I opened the Vic so I could specialize in Victorian drama. I love the wit of Wilde, the range of Dickens, the demands of Gilbert and Sullivan, and the ambiance of the age." Patting a belly that was just beginning to pot, he finished, "Now I do what I always wanted to do. It's a constant struggle to find backers, but I love choosing shows and watching them from my original conception to reality."

"From what I've seen, you've done well. The people here seem content." She could think of a couple who weren't that content, but overall, it was true.

"I liked your sister," Marle said, shifting gears, "but as I said earlier, I never felt she would be tolerant of certain things. You seem different."

"I try to be tolerant." *Of what? Backstage seduction? Sexual harassment?*

Marle set his glass down, excitement obvious in his manner. Alarm bells began clanging in her head. "Come with me," he said, heading down the only hallway in the place, where it was obvious there would be a bedroom, maybe two, and a bath. Christy stayed where she was.

"Come on," he said insistently. "I won't bite. You have to see this."

Biting was the least of her worries. Reluctantly Christy followed, wondering how fast she could get out if necessary. They passed a bedroom in green and gold that was apparently Marle's. Opposite it was a bathroom decorated in lilac shades. Beyond that was a door he threw open with a flourish, his face betraying excitement and pride as he flipped the light on and revealed his treasures.

Inside were three long, metal clothes racks filled with period dresses, sequined evening gowns, fluffy peignoirs, and assorted feminine accessories. The colors ranged from shocking orange to shiny black, and the items crowded against each other, big skirts bulging out the sides, long skirts trailing the floor, and high necks rising above their hangers. The array was as varied and elegant as anything she'd seen in the wardrobe area.

Marle beamed as Christy's eyes widened. "I need the advice of someone who understands costume," he said, waving at the array. "I just don't know which of these suits my complexion and body style."

Christy stood absolutely still for a few moments, staring at the racks of clothing. Finally she said, "Well, I think we can reject the pink one right off. Your complexion just isn't right for pastels."

Chapter Twelve

It was four a.m. when Cassie woke and looked at the clock beside the bed. Early for a meeting, but she guessed time was of no real importance here. It was merely another comfort provided to the guests, the illusion of normalcy. After washing her face and brushing her hair, which really didn't need it, she made her way to Nancy's office and knocked.

"Come in."

Nancy was sitting behind her desk as usual, dressed in lavender this time. A single file folder—hers, Cassie guessed—lay off to one side of the desktop. She realized she'd never seen another client or other work. Nancy always seemed to be waiting just for her.

One look apparently revealed everything. "You have questions, Cassie. Please, sit."

She sat, the comfortably padded chair and the plush carpet underfoot fairly shouting solidity that she knew was a lie. "How did I get here?" Her tone was more belligerent than she'd intended.

Nancy answered honestly. "I'm afraid I can't answer that."

Cassie covered her mouth with a hand for a moment to quell her quivering lips. Questions abounded, but she ordered herself to think before she spoke. "You don't, like, know everything?"

"There's a lot to know."

That made sense, sort of. "Can you tell me how I got to be here since I'm not, um, I don't—" As she fumbled for words, Nancy stepped in.

"You feel we've made a mistake."

Cassie felt like a fool. Who was she to question Eternity? Still, she had to be sure. "I haven't been to church in years, not since my mother died. And I don't fast during Lent. I don't tithe. I don't even own a rosary anymore."

"You're talking about the *things* of belief, Cassie."

"I'm not even close to being as good as my sister is. I don't—"

"Deserve to be here?" Nancy leaned forward. "Honestly, that's not our department, either. We're here to assure you understand that your earthly life is over. We try to make your transition pleasant. We have nothing to do with what comes before or after."

"You're just the messengers."

Apparently angels had no ear for sarcasm, because Nancy merely looked at her blankly. "I suppose that's one way to put it."

Folding her hands together to keep them still, Cassie said, "I was told you had to think and act in certain ways to get here."

Nancy nodded. "I've heard a lot about the rules of earth. The rules here are different."

"You're telling me no one on earth really understands how things work."

"One client told me that seeing eternity from earth is like peeping at the sun through a pinhole while wearing dark glasses. I rather liked the simile." Nancy leaned toward her. "You heard all your life that life and death are mysteries, haven't you?"

"Yes." Cassie recalled her mother quoting a favorite passage of scripture: "For now we see through a mirror dimly..."

"The wisest men and women on earth recognize the limitations of human intellect and acknowledge the possibility of a power beyond their comprehension." Nancy spoke softly, with no condescension or censure.

Cassie recalled the words of a Bengali philosopher she'd studied while trying to come to grips with her mother's untimely death: "Death is not extinguishing the light," he'd said. "It is putting out the lamp because the dawn has come."

Things began to make sense. If even the greatest thinkers of mankind admitted their lack of understanding of life and death, reward and punishment, it might be that she, a less-than-great thinker, had misjudged herself. Or maybe she'd misjudged Eternity.

"If I'm here, then I'm a candidate for going on?"

Nancy's smile was beautiful, as if she'd been waiting for her client to come to that very idea. "Of course you are, Cassie. Of course you are."

CHRISTY SLEPT UNTIL NINE, unheard of in the life she'd led just a week ago. As she rested, the late-evening scene at Marle's replayed in Seamus' head. Hard as he tried, he could not make it stop.

He'd jumped from Donna to Christy after the performance and ended up in Albert Marle's apartment, looking at a room full of women's clothing.

"No!" Christy had said to Albert firmly. "You should never wear lime green. It's just too sharp against your skin."

Marle had looked at the second gown she'd rejected regretfully. "I like the line of it. And it was quite expensive."

Christy put her hands on her hips. "You did ask for my input."

"I did." He'd draped the gown over a chair with others, an eggplant-colored silk with what she said was too much décolletage, a brown peignoir she dubbed muddy-looking, and the heavy pink dress she'd rejected first.

Seamus had seldom enjoyed an evening less, though he was impressed by Christy Parker's calm acceptance of Marle's little secret and her confident appraisal of his wardrobe. By the time she'd finished advising him on accessorizing and explained the benefits of quality undergarments, and by the time the director had asked a dozen fashion questions Seamus could not imagine a man considering, much less putting into words, he was not just ready to jump; he was desperate to. But there was nowhere to go, no one but the two of them, chatting about how fabrics drape and how shades of color matter. Seamus didn't sleep on earth, but last night had been his personal nightmare.

Christy finally woke, remarkably unfazed by the revelations of the night before. Seamus wasn't sure whether that was admirable or depressing.

When she reached the theatre, she went directly upstairs to her workroom, and he had no chance to find a new host for several hours. She bent over the sewing machine, concentrating on the costume she was making. When she went downstairs to find the woman who'd be wearing it, Seamus looked for a chance to jump to someone new.

As she descended to the main level, he sensed a rise in Christy's interest level. Two men stood in the lobby, one a stranger to Seamus and the other Henry Spellman. At first he thought Christy's interest was piqued by Spellman, but it was the other man. *John Damen*, her thought supplied.

Damen said a few words to Spellman then intercepted Christy at the bottom of the stairs.

"I came for that lunch you promised."

As she silently berated herself for neglecting her hair all morning, Seamus deduced that Christy liked this man. Thoughts of the non-existent Dora costume were brushed aside. "I guess I can get away for a while."

When he smiled, Seamus felt her temperature rise a notch. "Okay. Get your coat."

"Can we go somewhere close? I have a lot to do, and the matinee starts at two."

Seeing where this was headed, Seamus tuned out. Mating rituals had no interest for him. Besides, there was something else going on, something he hadn't experienced before. It was as if the air around him vibrated, sending out a low hum of activity that was familiar yet alien. What was it?

As Christy moved away from Damen, the odd feeling receded. She hurried up the steps, scooped up her coat, her purse, and a hat. She put the hat on, glanced at her reflection in the mirror, and dragged it off again, instead running a brush over her hair and plumping up the sides. After she buttoned the coat, unbuttoned two buttons, and buttoned them again, Seamus thought, *Enough, already!*

Go to lunch!

DAMEN AND CHRISTY went to the same café Inspector Nordman had taken her to a few days before. Her mood today was different. After Christy ordered a wrap and Damen a roast beef sandwich, the two of them reminisced about their shared past and caught each other up on the intervening years. "With Dad and Mom both gone," she told John, "there wasn't much in Fairfield for me, and I think Cassie knew that. She'd invited me to visit, but judging from the amount of my favorite foods stockpiled in her apartment, I think she planned to invite me to stay with her for a while."

"She was always taking care of you," John said.

"I think she felt a little guilty leaving me to take care of Dad. Cassie always thought of me as the good twin and herself as the not-so-good one, but you know she was a great person, always generous." Christy waved a hand. "After high school, I had no desire to leave Fairfield, and Dad and I got along well together. It's only since he died I realized I was hiding there, avoiding decisions about my life. Cassie didn't take advantage of me; I just needed more time to grow up than she did."

"I took advantage of her that day." John bit into a crunchy pickle. "I think she suspected my motives when I sent her inside for soda."

Christy smiled. "She knew something had happened, but I wouldn't tell. It was the only secret I ever kept from her." For some reason it had been important to Christy to keep their kiss to herself. It was fine with her when, some months later, Cassie had confessed to "making out" with Toby Ryan, becoming the first of them to experience romance, or so she thought.

Pulling herself back to the present, Christy said, "When they offered me Cassie's job, I decided to try it. So far it's not as scary as I'd expected." Glancing at her feet, she chuckled. "I do have to go home soon, though. Since I didn't plan to stay, I didn't bring some things I need, like my boots."

"You don't have a car?"

"Sure I do. It's at the train station in Barrie."

John put his sandwich down and took a drink. "I could drive you up there. You can get your car, and I'll follow you to Fairfield and drive you back here after you pick up the things you need."

"Oh, no," she began, but then she stopped. "Would you?"

"Isn't the theatre closed on Mondays? We could go tomorrow."

She thought about it. "I can't. I've got this big thing to get done, and I have no idea how I'm going to do it." She told John the story of the dress she was supposed to be making that was so far nothing more than a pencil sketch. When she finished, he was silent for a moment, and Christy chided herself for boring him. What man wanted to hear about vengeful actresses and Victorian dresses?

When he spoke, John sounded tentative. "I know nothing, so if this sounds dumb, just ignore it. But remember the Halloween costume you made one year? It was just an old dress you found in the attic, but you turned it into Queen Elizabeth or somebody."

"Marie Antoinette." She'd forgotten it, but the memory returned as he spoke. The dress had been plain, but she'd turned it into something special. The thought of that refashioned garment brought another thought, and Christy smiled. "John, I think you just saved my life, or at least my job."

"Then we can go north tomorrow?"

It would mean working late tonight, but she thought she could do it. She needed to go to Fairfield, she told herself, and she wanted to go with John. "If you let me pay for the gas. And lunch, of course."

"Sure," he agreed. "I intend to eat a lot, too, so look out."

Finished eating, Christy sat back in her chair. "It's your turn, John Damen. Tell me what happened in your life after Fairfield."

"Well," he said, "For that first year, nothing good. My mom was broke; that's why we moved to Mason's Bridge. Mom had an aunt there who let us live with her." His eyes darkened for a moment. "Aunt Lilly wasn't much for half-grown boys, but Mom got a job at a restaurant, and that's where she met the town's police chief. He'd been divorced for several years and took most of his meals at the diner. He liked her, and better yet, he took a liking to me." He smiled shyly. "I went from being the kid nobody wanted to being the police chief's son. It does wonders for a guy's self-confidence."

Christy nodded understanding, and he went on. "Mom

died when I was seventeen; the cigarettes finally got to her. That left me and Keith, my stepdad. He got me interested in being a cop and helped me get into the training program for the O.P.P."

"You're a cop?"

He gave her a comic salute. "Recently graduated from the academy and currently assigned to traffic."

"And you're helping investigate the hit-and-run in Mason's Bridge?"

"My stepdad asked the brass if it was okay for me to snoop on my time off." He shrugged. "Mostly I'm helping him cover all the bases." Scooting his chair back, he asked, "Shall we go?"

SEAMUS WAS PLEASED that Christy had met an old friend. Her fondness for John Damen was a good thing, easing the pain of her sister's death a bit. A job to keep her busy was a good antidote for grief, but a handsome guy taking her to lunch was better.

He noted, however, that Damen turned the conversation away from the hit-and-run a little too quickly. There was more to it than he was admitting. For his own part, Seamus was finding it hard to concentrate. The odd feeling had returned when Christy and Damen left the theatre together, and he tried to decide where it came from. It had to be Damen, though he seemed normal enough. Christy certainly saw nothing wrong with him. So why the aura that felt like electricity flowing out of him and into Seamus' head?

"I feel sorry for the people who were hit," Christy said as they left the restaurant. "What kind of person doesn't stop when—"

He tuned out again, knowing well the kind of person who could leave another to die.

The thing that was bothering him wouldn't go away. Seamus told himself to concentrate on something else, let his subconscious work on what it was, and an explanation would arise. Nothing came to him, and the thing was still there.

As they walked back to the Vic, Christy said, "Kim Snyder never struck me as a small town girl."

"I think she tries to put it as far behind her as possible, which is probably why she didn't tell anyone where she was going," John replied.

"Except Henry."

"Right." He didn't pursue the subject of Cassie's erstwhile boyfriend. "It was the first time Kim had been home in years. I guess she and her mother made some sort of truce for the sister's wedding." He rubbed a hand over the back of his neck. "From what I hear, she did her best to outshine the bride, arriving dressed to kill."

"With a semi-famous actor as escort." Christy's tone was sarcastic.

"All designed to irritate Mommy, who dominated Kim until she escaped to Toronto."

Christy sighed. "A stage mother, huh? No wonder Kim's so hard to get along with."

"What do you know about Spellman?"

"I shouldn't judge," Christy answered, "but he was Cassie's boyfriend, so why did he go away for the weekend with Kim?"

Damen tapped his lip with a finger. "He was seeing Cass? I picked up at the Vic that Kim lured him away from someone else, but nobody mentioned a name."

"Honestly, I don't know what caused their breakup."

Christy returned to the reason for John's initial visit. "So you came to ask if either of them saw anything that night?"

Damen shrugged. "Yeah. But Kim says they didn't stay at her parents' house."

Christy grimaced. "I heard that. They stayed at some inn."

"If they never went to Kim's house, they weren't on the road where it happened."

She met John's gaze. "I don't suppose their word on that clears them as suspects."

He smiled. "It does not. But I went out to Spellman's place and had a look at his car. It's fine, and there would have to have been some damage."

"It's a dead end, then."

"Right." Damen was silent for a few moments, his expression sober. "I'm really sorry about Cassie. She was a great person."

"I miss her a lot," Christy said. Seamus heard her thought: *It's nice to talk to someone who knew her well, someone from the days when we were inseparable.*

They'd reached the Vic, and John paused with his hand on the door, possibly deciding whether to say something.

Finally, he touched Christy's arm lightly. "I'm glad I found you again, and I hope there are better days ahead for you."

"I'll second that," she replied. He opened the door, and she went inside, turning back to smile at him once more before the theatre claimed her attention.

Seamus thought the presence he was feeling got stronger when Damen's hand touched Christy, but its source didn't get any clearer. What was that sizzle in the air?

Chapter Thirteen

Christy returned to work, her thoughts divided between John Damen (*So nice!*) and Henry Spellman (*What a creep!*). Seamus had intended to jump to Spellman, but that was not to be. The actor was nowhere to be seen, and besides, Christy's growing suspicion that he'd treated her sister badly made Seamus worry she might stab him with a pair of scissors if he came close.

No. Christy could never stab anyone. The worst Spellman would ever get from her was a hard stare.

Seamus settled for Donna as a host and ended up spending an hour in the box office. As she worked, he picked up bits that interested him from conversations she had with others. When the subject of Henry came up, Donna told the actress helping her fold programs, "Loser! Cassie's home for her dad's funeral and he's off screwing Kim, for Pete's sake!"

Seamus wondered briefly if Kim and Cassie had gotten into a fight that resulted in Cassie's death. It didn't seem likely. The fatal wound had undoubtedly been caused by the guillotine set piece, which was not a weapon someone might pick up in the midst of a struggle. Though Cassie had probably been hurt by Henry's betrayal, he didn't think she was the type to confront Kim. According to Donna, she'd blamed Henry for straying, not Kim for playing the siren. Still, he thought he'd spend some time with Kim to see if pure jealousy might spur her to attack Henry's former girlfriend.

At one-thirty the box office clerk came in, allowing Donna to head to the dressing room and get ready for the performance. As she passed Kim, Seamus jumped to her.

It was quite an adjustment. Kim's brain fairly boiled with thoughts of how unappreciated she was. She hated the secondary roles she played. She burned with a desire to be wealthy and famous. She longed to show her mother she could be successful without her, both on the stage and in life. And she despised almost everyone she worked with. Seamus found being inside Kim's head a little like standing against a wall and being pelted with kitchen gadgets.

He followed his usual procedure, settling in quietly in order to cause the least disturbance possible, but Kim didn't react to his presence with mild distress, as most hosts did. She reacted with waves of anger that seemed to pull Seamus backward and forward, making him, for the first time ever, more nauseated than his host. As soon as one hateful thought began, another overtook it. *Neen wouldn't know how to manage a stable! They should pay Beverly to stay off the stage! Marle, you pompous, overblown pervert!* and when Christy passed with a costume for another actress, Kim's thoughts screamed *What a hick!* followed by a snippet about Cassie—*deserved what she got.*

The twins reminded Kim of the small-town roots she wanted desperately to forget. *Why in hell did I go back there?* she asked herself. *Should have stayed away.* Seamus learned that the return to her home town had sprung from two purposes, first, to show off her success to her friends and family, and second, to ensnare Henry Spellman. He sensed regret in her mind now, as if neither result had been worth the effort.

Kim repeatedly pushed something worrisome into her sub-conscious. Seamus guessed it stemmed from the fact she'd deliberately stolen Cassie Parker's boyfriend while Cassie dealt with her father's death. As Kim was made up to look like the aged Miss Pross, she fumed inwardly, hating the character, the makeup woman, and Tarcie Starpon, who had the lead role Kim wanted. Seamus also picked up repeated rueful threads concerning Mason's Bridge and Henry Spellman. Maybe she'd realized the old truth that a woman who steals a man from another is likely to lose him the same way.

At one point he heard a thread of worry about her parents, but he couldn't figure out a reason. Her mother had disapproved of Henry, who'd apparently gotten drunk at the reception and become arrogant and overbearing. Not the impression Kim had hoped for. Kim was thinking her mother should keep her mouth shut, but then her thoughts took a jump, moving on to someone else she didn't like.

Overall, Seamus learned only what he already knew: the inside of a self-centered person's head is an unpleasant place to be. While Kim was volatile, he didn't see her lying in wait to swing a set piece at Cassie in order to keep her hold on Henry. Kim was nothing if not self-confident, and having won the man she wanted, she had no doubt she could hang onto him.

He spent the rest of the performance with Tarcie

Starpon, who played Lucy Manette. She was the center of everything. The audience loved her, the other actors deferred to her, and the crew made it a point to clear the way wherever she went. Seamus had never been associated with royalty but guessed Tarcie came close, at least in the tiny world of the Vic. Knowing what some of them thought of her as they smiled and flattered, he saw how precarious her position at the top of the pecking order was. Tarcie was their queen, but many hoped to see her fall, and plenty of them wanted to take her place.

At Ruth's urging, Cassie agreed to go to dinner that evening in the dining room. Dress was formal, and Ruth insisted on accompanying her to Raiment, the ship's clothing store, and overseeing her choice of a gown. "It'll be nice to see someone who does justice to Elaine's choices," Ruth said on the way. "She outfits everybody, but you make a better looking corpse than most of us do."

For a moment the comment shocked her, but having done her share of outfitting people who required extensive camouflage, Cassie chuckled. *Get over it*. She told herself.

Get on with it.

Elaine, a willowy blond, stood behind a counter and before a huge rack of clothing that rotated at the press of a button. After looking Cassie over, she stopped and started the machine until she'd located two dresses. "Will either of these work?" she asked, laying them out on the counter.

With expertise gained over years of sewing, Cassie could tell the garments were excellently made and so beautiful she could hardly choose between them. "That one," Ruth said decisively. Her recommendation was bright orange, a color Cassie would never have imagined wearing, but something in her mind urged, *Enjoy what's offered.*

"Why not?" she said aloud, taking the dress. Elaine immediately pressed a second button, causing an array of shoes to pass under a window in the counter. "Those," Cassie said after a few dozen pairs of shoes appeared and disappeared.

Elaine stopped the machine, handed over the shoes, and added a bag of accessories that included a stunning onyx necklace that would fall perfectly into the gown's neckline. "You'll look wonderful in that."

Her enthusiasm was contagious, and Cassie wondered, if

this was indeed the afterlife, what place did the workers have in it? Were they paying off earthly debts, or were they volunteers? Elaine seemed happy in her work, so she guessed working was optional.

Next Ruth made her choices, a peach-colored gown with accessories that added, as she requested, "Lots of sparkle, please. I've got to sit next to this pretty young thing."

The two women left Raiment together, carrying their bundles of finery. Cassie's spirits rose a little, possibly from the combination of having a friend in this strange place and having a new outfit to wear. She'd lost everything, but she was beginning to accept that there might be something more important than what "everything" implied on earth. She was in the company of someone she liked and admired, and she had a dress finer than any she'd ever owned. Touching the satiny fabric of her evening gown, she thought, *If this is heaven, they know how to get a girl on their side!*

Dinner conversation was a little unnerving, however. Everyone at the table accepted his or her death as fact, some with good reason. One man recalled the semi that turned over in front of him and the flash of realization there was no way he'd steer clear of the accident. Several of them were elderly, and without exception professed themselves relieved to be done with old age. "They can call them the Golden Years all they want," a woman remarked. "Nothing golden about disintegrating, bit by bit."

"Oh, I loved life," another woman argued. "If you'd asked me if I was ready, I'd have said no. But knowing now what I didn't know then, I have to say this is better." She turned to her mound of battered shrimp with enthusiasm.

"Nobody did me any favors back there," one rather grumpy man announced. "They tell what a caring society we have, but sit in a nursing home for a day or two and tell me if it's worth staying alive. I begged my kids to let me die in my own home, but they wouldn't hear of it."

"I'm sure your children meant well," Ruth said soothingly.

"They did," he agreed. "For my own good, they put me in a holding pen where I could play Bingo and wait to die in complete safety." He stabbed a piece of fish with his fork. "At least a fall down the basement steps wouldn't have taken five years."

Cassie saw a few heads nod in agreement. She'd never

thought of death as a relief, but then, she'd never been old, sick, and dependent. Dying young was a tragedy, to be sure, but so was outlasting the joy of life.

WHEN THE EVENING PERFORMANCE WAS OVER, Christy neatened the prop table, setting fans, gloves, and reticules in their assigned places. Finished, she turned to find John Damen watching her. "Hi."

"You came to the show!

"Twice," he said, holding up two fingers. "I saw it this afternoon and liked it, so I came back. I figured you'd be busy all day, but you might be free for a drink now."

She felt herself blushing. "I'd love to."

After she retrieved her coat from upstairs, they went out into the frosty night, walking a few blocks to a bar called Teddy's that someone at the Vic had recommended. When they stepped from the crisp night air into the overheated bar, Christy saw several people she knew. They turned to greet her, some still wearing their theatrical makeup, most with drinks already in hand. It felt good to be recognized, to be part of the company.

They made the rounds, speaking to almost everyone. John told a few people what he'd liked about their performances, and Christy was pleased to find he sounded neither lame nor tongue-tied. He told Beverly, who played Madame Defarge, that he'd been struck by her accent. "Using Cockney dialect is a great idea."

"Thanks. After I saw it done in *Les Miz*, I argued my case until Albert agreed. I think it gives a sense of social class that a phony French accent wouldn't." Wrinkling her nose, she added, "Albert wasn't hard to convince. It was his niece who objected."

"Who's Albert's niece?" Christy asked.

"Tarcie, who knows absolutely everything about the theatre. Peasants like us can't comprehend what she knows!" Beverly put on a snooty expression like Tarcie at her most imperious.

Christy was putting things together. "Tarcie is Albert's niece!"

"Yeah, and she's also a pain. So protective of his precious reputation!" Beverly looked around at the others, whose grins indicated they shared her opinion.

Christy thought of her visit to Marle's apartment. "His

reputation. I see."

Beverly leaned in and whispered, "She thinks nobody knows."

"Oh." Christy glanced at the other actors, who chuckled knowingly.

"What?" John asked, sensing the shared secret.

"Nothing," she said, giving him a look that signaled he should drop the subject. Even if the company knew about their director's eccentric collection, she didn't think it was right to share that outside the group.

Now she knew why Tarcie had accosted her. She'd have to find a way to let the actress know she'd keep Albert's secret, though she wondered how much it mattered in today's world. Trying on women's clothing was no crime, and most would consider it a harmless peccadillo. And really, was it any of Tarcie's business?

Excusing themselves, John and Christy settled into a booth apart from the others. After ordering cheese sticks and beer, they continued their conversation from earlier, comparing favorite movies, songs, and groups, and recalling childhood stories. John again expressed delight with the show. "I haven't seen much live theatre," he confessed, "but I really enjoyed tonight."

"You should come to the new show," Christy urged. "If you like Dickens, that is."

"I don't know if I do. Aside from *A Christmas Carol* and today, I'm clueless."

She laughed. "Where were you when Mrs. Cooley was extolling the virtues of Dickens in seventh grade English?"

"Watching you, probably. You were so beautiful when you were listening, with that little frown of concentration, like you were trying to remember every single word the teachers said."

She chose to ignore the compliment. "Well, we'll have to educate the Dickens into you!"

His eyes met hers. "I'm okay with that."

At a little after one, they left the pub, Christy leading John by the hand as she said goodnights to those still gathered around the bar. Several women eyed her with jealousy. As far as they knew, she'd snared the attention of a handsome man only days after they'd met. They must have wondered why, with all the gregarious and gorgeous women in the company, he'd been attracted to their quiet little wardrobe mistress.

Let them wonder. Christy didn't feel like telling anyone she'd known John Damen for years. Their childhood friendship was a strong base, but she thought they'd begun to build something in the present as well. When they pulled up in front of her apartment, she leaned over and kissed him on the cheek. "Goodnight, John Damen," she said, sliding out of the car. "I've missed you all these years."

Christy watched a little TV, brushed her teeth, and wrapped up in a blanket on the couch, being so far unable to sleep in her sister's bed. It took a while for her to drop off to sleep, but when her breathing slowed and her mind stopped whirling with the day's events, she slept. That was when Seamus got the shock of his day.

"Are you there, Cross-back?"

"Who's that?"

"You are a cross-back, right?"

"Yeah. "The light was beginning to dawn. "I'm Seamus."

"Nice to meet you, Seamus. I'm Ronnie."

The voice, low and vibrant, didn't sound like a Ronnie. It was definitely feminine. "Ronnie?"

"Veronica, if you must know. I prefer Ronnie."

Recalling a Mildred who'd refused to be called Millie, he shuddered mentally. That relationship had been rocky most of the way along.

"Ronnie, are you hosting with John Damen?"

"Yes. It was quite a surprise when I felt your presence."

"How did you know?"

"That there was another cross-back in the area? One of the others described getting a tingly sense of something weird."

"Really? What are the chances?"

"I'm guessing it's pretty rare." She gave him a few seconds to process before continuing. "I'm looking into the death in the hit-and-run. How about you?"

"My client died at the theatre a few nights ago, but she doesn't believe she's dead."

"She doesn't believe it? How does she explain the ship and Mike and Nancy?"

"Wouldn't even talk about it. Mike thought if she had details, she might believe it."

"So you aren't investigating a murder?"

"I haven't found a motive for anyone to murder Cassie.

In fact, I was thinking of wrapping it up." That prospect wasn't likely now. Another cross-back was intriguing.

"Cassie, that's the sister to the girl Damen likes, Christy?"

"Yeah. Are you getting anywhere with the hit-and-run?"

"It's slow. I started with Chief Damen, watching while he interviewed family and friends. I didn't get the sense any of them was guilty, so I decided to come with young John and see what he learned in Toronto."

"What's he thinking?"

"Right now he's just gathering information. For a Liver, he's pretty open-minded."

"Liver?"

"It's what we call them." When Seamus didn't answer, she added defensively, "It's not derogatory. It's just what cross-backs say when they trade stories, you know?"

"I guess."

Ronnie's tone changed slightly. "I've heard of you, Seamus. You're kind of a legend, kind of a mystery. They all talk about you, but nobody knows you very well."

"I'm not much for mixing."

"That's what they say. They also say you're really good at this job."

"I just do what I'm asked to do."

"And you've been doing it for ages." She chuckled. "One advantage to being dead is we'll never get too old for the job. Anyway, I hear you've got it all, intelligence, guts, experience, and dedication."

"You're making me blush."

Ronnie laughed. "Here's a bulletin for you, old man. I've got intelligence, guts, and dedication too. I don't have as much experience as you, but I'm pretty darned good. They say you don't like working with others, but I think we should pool our information. I promise I can keep up."

Seamus liked Ronnie's voice and her straight-on approach. She'd laid it right out: she admired him but didn't necessarily defer to him. Recalling his recent yen for a partner, he thought her offer wasn't bad. If they teamed up, he'd have someone to talk to, and they might help each other with their respective cases.

"Okay," he said, keeping his voice toneless. "I guess we can see how things work out."

Chapter Fourteen

THE NEXT MORNING as she made her way to breakfast, Cassie saw the Orlando Bloom look-alike again. When their eyes met, she realized he'd been waiting for her.

"Good morning, Cassie, I'm Mike."

The guy in the vintage suit had said an angel named Mike sent him. Since both Mike and Nancy looked like movie stars, Cassie guessed they took on forms familiar to each client, someone comfortable. She wondered what Mike really looked like, but it was probably beyond her comprehension, like everything else here.

She no longer felt anger toward them. Acceptance had taken over. "Hello, Mike."

"Ruth tells me you're coming along well."

"Ruth?" Another synapse connected in her brain, and she got it. "You sent her to me."

Mike smiled, but there was no condescension in it. "Everyone needs help with it. Sometimes we can provide the help; other times we try to locate those who can."

They'd done what they had to do, she realized. She'd been unwilling to believe in her own mortality, and they'd proved it to her as gently as possible.

"The first guy you sent. Was he—"

Raising a hand, Mike chuckled. "Seamus wasn't there to convince you. He has his own set of ethics, and he didn't want to go to work for you without your knowledge."

"Work for me?"

"He's what we call a cross-back. He goes back to life to investigate deaths like yours, deaths where questions remain."

Back to life! The phrase caught her attention, and Mike added hastily, "They don't really go back to life. They're sort of a presence inside someone living."

"Like ghosts?"

"That's as close to understanding it as most get," Mike said. "Anyway, Seamus is investigating what happened to you, to see if it was an accident or...something else."

"You mean murder?" She was shocked. "Nobody would murder me!"

"It that's true, Seamus will find it out. It's just that he's been gone a while.”

“You think he found something to investigate?”

“He’s probably just being thorough.” Mike shrugged. “We didn’t know how to help you, but we thought if you knew exactly what happened, you’d be better able to accept your death.”

“Oh, I’ve accepted it,” Cassie told him, her voice holding only a tiny tinge of regret. “The only thing this Seamus guy can do to help me now is let me know how my sister is doing without me.”

MONDAY MORNING, John Damen picked Christy up at her place so early that the sky was still lit by street lamps. His sporty Camaro was less than sure-footed on the newly-fallen snow, but Damen guided it expertly onto the 400 Motorway, which had already been cleared of snow. “We should be there by nine-thirty,” he told her.

They were quiet on the drive up to Barrie. Christy wasn’t much for chatting first thing in the morning, and she guessed John wasn’t either. At the train station’s parking area, she pointed out her car, and he helped her clear the snow and ice from it, taking his time and cleaning the headlights, taillights, and side windows thoroughly. They waited until the defrosters had done their work, their breath puffing white into the air as they spoke of winter things. Christy was pleased that John didn't give her driving instructions. She'd dated men who thought women, even women born and raised in Ontario, couldn't comprehend such things as black ice and skid correction.

When her car was warm, Christy took the lead, and they left Barrie, turning west and traveling through a number of small towns. When they reached Fairfield, she glanced in the rearview mirror, wondering what John was thinking as he returned to the place where he'd once lived.

Christy drove through town then followed a succession of country roads, each narrower than the one before it as snow banks crowded them on both sides. Almost at the end of the road was the Parker farm, a yellow brick, two-story house with a stately but largely unused front entrance with white wooden pillars and an oval window in the door. Behind the house were several outbuildings, a large barn, a chicken coop, a silo, and various sheds for storage. Christy noticed signs of decay on several of them. She'd been too busy in the last year to see to their upkeep.

The drive was unplowed since she'd left, but the snow wasn't very deep. She drove up next to the back door and got out as John pulled in behind her.

"I don't think one thing's changed in Fairfield," he said as he approached her, feet crunching through the crusty snow.

"Don't be silly," she chided with mock severity. "They painted the insurance company office last year and the gas station on the corner has new pumps as of 2010."

"I apologize," he said with a grin. "How could I have missed all that progress?"

"This won't take long." She opened the storm door, making a perfectly flat arc in the drifted snow, and unlocked the back door.

He waved a hand to dismiss any thought of hurry. "We've got all day."

"Would you like to come in?" she asked, belatedly chiding herself for rudeness.

"I'll wait here." He tilted his head a little to one side. "Unless you want company."

She didn't, because she had no idea how walking into her

lifelong home was going to affect her. If she started crying, she didn't want John to see. "I can handle it."

Unlocking the door, Christy went inside. The air was already stuffy, and the house so quiet that the tick of the kitchen clock sounded like someone had turned the volume up to full. The house felt strangely alien, like she hadn't been there for years. Had it really been only a few days since she left?

They'd removed the hospital bed after Dad died, and the corner where it had been looked starkly empty. This had been home, but she was the only part of it still living. Now it was just a house full of memories.

She located her boots, a couple of items of clothing she wanted, and some toiletries, put them into a bag, and went back outside. John was standing in the drive, hands in his coat pockets, staring at the barn with a pensive expression. When she joined him, tossing her things into the back seat of his car, he said, "That's a place I've thought about a lot over the years. It was like I was someone else when I was here."

Christy smiled fondly at the old building. "Yeah, we spent a lot of time in that barn."

"Do you remember the forts?"

She turned to him, eyes widening. "Dad got so mad when he fell into one! Bales of hay make great walls, but they don't work quite so well for a roof."

"Is the block and tackle still there, where we'd swing from one side to the other?"

She regarded him mischievously. "Want to look?"

"Of course!"

"First let me put these on." Sitting sideways in the car seat, she pulled off her shoes and tossed them into the back. Pulling on her boots, she tucked her pant legs into the tops and tied the laces.

After closing the car door, Christy glanced at John's running shoes and ordered, "Follow me and walk in my tracks, or you'll get your socks all wet."

"Yes, ma'am," he said with exaggerated meekness.

Breaking through the snow with each step, Christy led the way to the ancient, hip-roofed barn. Its red color was starting to fade, and she made a mental note to see what it would cost to have someone paint it. The thought brought her up short. Who cared if the building turned gray or even collapsed to the ground? Her dad had been the last of his family, and now she was the last of hers. She'd never grow produce to sell at the farm markets in the area, never plant corn or wheat or soybeans on this land. The barn was no good to anyone. Still, her Dad wouldn't have wanted it to decay. *It won't hurt to get an estimate.*

John opened the barn door by pushing it along a metal track, producing a squeal of protest that added lubricating the hinges to Christy's list of what needed to be done. The smell of old hay drifted out, though hay was no longer stored there. Instead there was a collection of rejected machinery, household items, and a tarp-covered shape that took up most of the middle section.

"What's that?" John asked.

"I should have known a guy would notice," Christy replied. "It's an old car Dad inherited from his brother. He was always going to fix it up and sell it, but he never did."

"What kind of car?"

"A 1970 Chevelle."

"What?" His voice rose.

She frowned. "I think that's right. Maybe there were letters, like SS?"

His face froze. "Really?" A second later he asked, "Can I

look?"

"Sure."

Christy spent the next fifteen minutes saying things like, "Uh-huh," and "Really?" in response to John's animated comments.

"Did you know this is a 454?"

"Really?"

"Christy, this is a classic."

"Uh-huh."

"Do you see the body? It's in really good shape."

"Uh-huh."

"And the frame seems solid too."

"Really."

She finally wandered away, exploring the barn as John crawled over, under, and through the car, inspecting every part, at least it seemed so to her. She didn't really mind, because the barn, for some reason, felt more like home than the house had. Here she and Cass had played as children, often with their friend Johnny. Here they'd worked on projects with Mom and Dad, sorting potatoes into graded piles or polishing pumpkins to sell at a stand in town. And all those times, everywhere, she and Cassie had talked and talked and talked, about anything, everything, and nothing.

There was ticking overhead. The sun was warming the roof, causing it to expand and click against the nails that held the metal sheets in place. Looking up at the peak, twenty feet above her head, she located the pulley they used to swing from. There was no rope there now, but she glanced around, recreating in her mind the daring feats they'd done, daring in the minds of ten-year-olds.

The windows at either end of the barn were high, almost at roof level. One of their favorite things had been jumping from those windows onto the piled bales of hay. As bales were removed and sold over the course of a year, the distance to their landing spot grew, and more courage was required to make the jumps. Cassie had always gone first, unafraid. Johnny had always matched her, and Christy had followed him, unwilling to be the chicken of the trio. Once Cassie'd done it, it was doable, and it was always a thrill when Christy finally let go and sailed through the air.

Together they'd climbed to every corner of the barn, like squirrels exploring their territory. She could almost feel the rough rope in her hands, sense the swing as her body hung suspended, and see the dirt floor spinning below.

Suddenly she missed her sister more than ever. She wanted to tell her she loved her and wanted to let her know about John, that she'd found him and he was every bit as sweet as she remembered.

The slam of a hood got her attention. John was wiping his hands on his jeans and grinning like a happy teenager. "This car is sweet."

"I guess that makes your trip up here worthwhile."

He picked up the tarp and spread it over the car, although he seemed reluctant to lose sight of it. "I'd have driven twice this distance to see a car like this."

"It's got no seats," she objected, but he gestured to indicate the insignificance of that. "It doesn't even run."

"Your dad emptied the gas tank, cleaned the carburetor, drained the oil, and put it up on blocks. He did everything right to preserve it; now it just needs work."

She felt her lips curve upward. "And you'd like to do this work?"

"I'd love to." He rubbed his neck with one hand. "But I can't afford it right now. I just got out of the academy, and—"

Christy laughed aloud. "I wasn't trying to sell it to you,

John!"

"I really would love to buy it. I just don't have a place to keep it, or the cash to get the stuff I'd need to get it in shape."

"Tell you what," she said. "This farm and this barn aren't going anywhere. When you're ready to own a '70 Chevelle, I'll sell it to you."

"Really?"

"Really."

"You could probably sell it now and get some cash."

"I'm so busy at the Vic, I don't have time to shop, so why do I need money?"

His expression had turned odd, and Christy thought she'd said something wrong. "I don't want the car," he said, and a note in his voice confirmed her misstep.

After a moment, she said casually, "It's up to you."

His next comment, made with eyes averted, seemed like a departure, but Christy made the connection. "Your family was always good to me."

"Because we liked you."

He looked at her then, and the question in his eyes spilled into words. "Not because you felt sorry for me? Not because my mother had no idea which of her boyfriends to name as my father?"

"Of course not!" Christy struggled to find the right words. "Because you're a good person. We all saw that in you, even my dad, who didn't like just anybody."

Her mother and Cass had seen how devastated Christy was when Johnny moved away, and they'd tried to make her feel better with extra kindnesses: a batch of her favorite cookies, a chore done before she got to it, and discussion of the mysteries of some so-called parents' behavior. Her father didn't seem to notice her pain at the time, but once, years later, he'd mentioned Johnny. She'd come downstairs dressed for a formal dance, twirling to show him the dress she'd made for the occasion.

"Nice." For Earl it was a big compliment. "Who's taking you to this dance?"

"Brian Waggoner," she replied, hiding a smile at the thought her father had failed to notice her main topic of conversation for the last three weeks.

"That Walter's boy?"

"Yes, Dad." Why did grown-ups always have to know a person's lineage?

"Seems all right." Earl leaned back, causing the ancient wooden kitchen chair to squeak in protest. "Would have been nice if Johnny Canby had stayed in town, though. He never thought he was better than everybody else, like the Waggoners tend to do."

He'd been right, of course. Before the evening was over, Brian Waggoner had insulted Christy in a dozen ways, the last being the assumption that because he'd bought her dinner and a corsage, she'd climb into the back seat of his car with him.

"I never felt sorry for you," she told John now. "We wished things could have been easier for you and your mother, but that isn't the same thing."

John thought about that. "You're the best kind of people, Chris. Do you know that?"

She blushed lightly. "There's nothing unusual about including an extra person at dinner."

"You'd be surprised. Some people's kindnesses have strings attached, or they're stained by *noblesse oblige*." He grinned, his humor restored. "In spite of all the free meals your mother fed me and the money your dad used to slip into my hand when I helped out with the farm work, I never thought anyone at your house was keeping a tally of what I owed in return."

Embarrassed, Christy returned to the original topic. "Well, if you want this car, you'll owe me whatever those sell-your-car websites say it's worth. It doesn't have to be soon."

He looked at the lump under its protective tarp. "That's really nice of you."

She waved the compliment away. "It's not a big deal."

John stepped closer. "It's a big deal to me."

The barn suddenly seemed warmer, and Christy found she couldn't look away from John Damen's eyes. He looked down at her for a moment, and then, without either of them making the choice, they were in each other's arms. The kiss was a surprise, yet it felt inevitable, as if they had been headed toward this moment since they met at the theatre. When they parted, he said firmly, "That had nothing to do with the car. I've wanted to do it all day."

She smiled and turned to go, reflecting that her heart felt much like it had in those long-ago days when she'd gathered her courage and swung across the barn: light as a bird, tingly with excitement, and giddy with delight.

Chapter Fifteen

CASSIE WAS SITTING on the deck when Ruth found her. "Let's walk," she said, and Cassie rose to join her. They made their way along the wide expanse, passing a game of canasta, a lively group at the shuffleboard court, and a group arguing the relative merits of their favorite basketball teams. Ruth seemed lost in thought, but Cassie didn't mind. It was pleasant just to be with her, to know she wasn't alone in all this.

They ambled, mostly in silence, until they came to what felt like the aft rail. It wasn't as if one felt an actual direction, but there was a slight sense that the ship traveled forward. They leaned on the rail, their arms resting on it loosely. After a few moments, Ruth spoke. "I've forgotten what my daughter looks like."

"It'll come back," Cassie assured. "When you're away from people, it's hard to recall details."

Ruth turned to face her. "No. It's not like that. I've

forgotten. She's not in there." She pointed vaguely to her forehead. Cassie didn't know what to say, but Ruth went on, "The longer you're here, the more you forget. Nancy says that's how it has to be. If we don't forget, we might never go on."

She meant to argue, but her friend's expression stopped her. "What happens if you stay here?"

"They give you a job, something to make you feel useful. I don't think it helps, though. You still forget who you were, the essence of your life." Ruth smiled grimly. "I've seen the ones with no memories. They're just going through the motions."

"Then you're going on?"

Ruth touched Cassie's shoulder. "I have some things to do yet, but soon I'll be ready."

Cassie wanted to beg her to stay. She didn't want to be alone on the ship with Perfect Nancy and Flawless Mike. She wanted real people like Ruth to talk to. Of course, what she really wanted was to go home, back where she belonged, to find her sister and her friends at—

With a jolt of horror, Cassie realized she couldn't remember the name of the theatre. And her sister...Christy.

At least she remembered her name! She knew Christy looked exactly like her and was a little too diffident. But she couldn't recall the sound of her voice or her smile. She couldn't remember.

CHRISTY ENDED UP putting her RAV4 in the barn next to the Chevelle. It took some doing to get it through the deep snow of the unplowed barnyard. They were both wet to the knees by the time they got it done, but at least the car was protected from the elements.

The ride back seemed shorter as Christy and John talked about all sorts of things. He was interested in her job, and she was fascinated by his stories of OPP training and his current work. When they got back to Christy's place, she didn't want their day together to end. Maybe it was their similar background and shared memories. Maybe it was the fact they'd both chosen to leave their small towns and jump into a larger pool to see if they could succeed. Maybe it was those warm brown eyes of his. Or maybe, she admitted, it was death, the recent loss of the two people she'd cared about most in this world. She'd been patient, accepting what life offered, but now she felt positively reckless. It wasn't always wise to wait for tomorrow. For some, tomorrow never came.

Damen seemed to catch her mood. "It was a good day, wasn't it?"

"It was."

He planted a kiss on her forehead. "I've missed you, Christy Parker."

She smiled up at him, and her eyes filled with promise. "Would you like to come in?"

"Well, that was embarrassing," Ronnie said a few hours later.

"Ummm." Seamus would have preferred it if she'd ignored the whole thing.

"It's different, being the guy."

"Ronnie—"

"Okay, I get it. But don't you ever compare, like between people? I mean, you smell garlic in Person A, and it smells one way, but for Person B, it's totally different."

Relieved that she'd moved to a topic less embarrassing

than sex in someone else's body, Seamus said, "You should try being inside a rat."

"What? That story is true?"

He chuckled. "They talk about it, do they?"

"You're a legend, like I said."

"Well, the rat was no fun, so I guess being a legend isn't all it's cracked up to be." He returned to business. "Damen didn't say much about your case today. Has he made progress toward finding the hit-and-run driver?"

"Not much in the way of hard evidence. But he thinks it was a guy from the theatre where your girl works, Henry Spellman."

"Spellman, huh? What's his reasoning?"

"The guy got really drunk that night. And he and Kim tell the story of their weekend in almost the exact words. That's usually a sign a story's been rehearsed."

"That's been my experience."

"The male victim was badly hurt, but he recalls opening his eyes and seeing a woman's shoes. He heard a voice from the car call out a name. He thought it was 'Jim,' but Damen thinks it could have been 'Kim.'"

"He checked Spellman's car for damage?"

"He did. The car's in good shape."

Seamus paused, letting something in his memory float back to consciousness. "What if Damen had evidence that Spellman recently had his car repaired?"

"That would change things," Ronnie said. "What have you got?"

He told her about seeing the repair slip on Cassie's desk. "It was gone after Spellman came to pick up his stuff." He clicked his tongue in disgust. "Kim's covering for him. I felt some worry in her mind, but she's one of those hosts you don't stay with any longer than you have to, you know?"

"Yeah, I've had a few of those. Brutal."

"Most times I like the living. Being a cross-back isn't like being alive, but it's something, you know?"

"I like that part too. And I like the idea of finding answers for clients that can't go on until they know." She asked, "Do you usually stick with one person or move around?"

"I move a lot. Pick up bits and pieces until I can zero in."

"I suppose I should do that more, but it's hard getting used to a new Liver—um, host—each time."

"Yeah. Some of them are pretty hard to stay with." He thought of Amy's self-centeredness and Kim's anger. "But then there are the ones who are nice or even fun." He told her about the young actor who'd sneaked into the theatre through an upstairs window. "Just full of youthful confidence and high spirits, that one."

"It's weird how their moods color the way they see things."

"Yeah," he agreed. "Christy's sad right now, but she's a positive person, so it's okay. I've seen some that can hardly function."

"You wish you could tell them that dying isn't so bad."

Seamus grunted. "The dying part can be bad." After a moment he added, "But you're right. I wish the people left behind could know the ones who've gone on are all right."

"Why is it such a big secret?" Her voice rose, and Seamus felt Christy shift, her sleep disturbed by the sound.

When she'd returned to sleep, he said, "How many would stay here when they could go there?"

Ronnie didn't answer, and he returned to business. "In the morning I'm going to remind Christy about the repair slip and hope she mentions it to Damen. Make sure he pays attention."

"I'll do my best."

Sometime later, Seamus heard Ronnie's voice again. "Do you realize that what we've figured out tonight makes your case more interesting?"

"My case?"

"If your girl Cassie saw that paper, she knew Spellman's car was in the shop. If Damen had asked her about the hit-and-run, she might've put two and two together."

"Why would he ask Cassie about an accident that happened miles away from here?"

"He wouldn't, but think about it. Chief Damen called Kim and said he was sending someone to the Vic to interview her and Spellman."

"Which makes me think the chief had his suspicions about their involvement."

"He did. Anyway, Spellman and Cassie fought about something that day, and their relationship came to an abrupt end."

"Because she came back to Toronto and found out about his weekend with Kim."

"Yeah. She was probably furious." Ronnie's tone revealed growing enthusiasm for her theory. "Let's say that somehow Cassie got hold of the work order for Spellman's car."

"His coat was at her apartment, and the paper looked crumpled, like it had been stuffed into a pocket." Seamus paused as Christy turned over in her sleep.

"Spellman had to be worried when he realized she had it." He imagined Ronnie counting her points on her fingers, though she was only a voice in this place and time. "A hit-and-run in Mason's Bridge on a night when Spellman had had plenty to drink; a cop on the way to the Vic to ask about it; and Spellman's angry ex-girlfriend with evidence that his car had recently been repaired. He must have felt he had to do something about one of those. Silencing Cassie was one possibility."

"He killed her so she couldn't spill the beans?"

Ronnie made an audible snort. "Spill the beans, Seamus? Who says that anymore?"

"I do." His tone was flat.

"Okay," she said, still chuckling. "Then I'm adding it to my repertoire. I love a detective with an ear for figurative language."

Chapter Sixteen

CASSIE WAS APPREHENSIVE when Ruth knocked on her door the next morning. Though she was glad her friend hadn't yet left her forever, she wasn't sure what she wanted for Ruth, or for herself, either.

The older woman was matter-of-fact. "I don't want to leave until I'm sure you're okay."

"I'll be fine." She tried for a confident tone, but it didn't come off well.

Ruth put out her hands in a plea for understanding. "I like you, Cassie. I feel like a rat for leaving you like this."

"You aren't leaving me. You're doing what you need to do." Cassie sighed. "I have to do the same, as soon as I figure out what it is."

Ruth nodded. "Come with me to the library. I want to return these books before I go."

"Sure." She doubted it mattered if a person returned books that were probably imaginary, but she understood

Ruth's desire to feel she'd finish things. Death was messy, coming for a person when he or she didn't expect it. Here, the choice was theirs. Eternity waited patiently for each of them.

The library was set up somewhat like the clothing store, with a counter and an attendant. Here, rather than racks of clothes, shelves of books rotated behind the desk, turning silently until the requested piece could be pulled from its place and handed to the reader. The rest of the room contained chairs of various types, everything from carrels to recliners to sofas. Some people sat reading novels, others leaned over large, hard-backed tomes laid out on tables. The man at the counter took Ruth's books with a polite smile. "What can I get for you today, Ruth?"

"Nothing, but thanks, Adam." His brows rose in surprise, but he didn't comment.

They turned away and Ruth surveyed the room, looking for a quiet place. A sectional couch sat empty in one corner, and she headed toward it. When they were seated, almost facing each other, Cassie tried to ease her friend's mind.

"Ruth, you know I had doubts. But I'm over them now."

Ruth was not quite satisfied. "You seemed a little angry

with Nancy before."

"There's just so much I don't understand," Cassie said, raising her hands in a helpless gesture. "And they won't tell us."

Ruth gave a dry chuckle. "Honestly, Cassie, I don't think they can."

"Why can't they?"

Chewing her bottom lip for a moment, Ruth asked, "Before you cut up a tomato, do you explain to it what you're doing and why?"

Cassie frowned. "I don't know what you mean."

Ruth leaned toward her and put a hand on her arm. "I mean that as long as we hold onto these selves, Ruth or Cassie or even Elvis, as long as we insist on keeping our human-ness, we're incapable of understanding what's beyond that. You said it yourself: we don't even know which questions to ask."

"But surely we could grasp the basics."

"I doubt it." Ruth shrugged good-naturedly. "We haven't got the capacity to understand God. That's why we try so hard to make God be like us." Putting both hands on her knees in a gesture that was probably more habitual than necessary, she rose. "Let's go. I'd like to look into the void one more time."

Cassie rose too, and they went onto the deck. Outside the ship the mists rolled, and Ruth sighed contentedly. "I have to say, it's a relief to have made the last decision I'll ever have to make."

Her words didn't sound dire or final or scary. They struck a chord. One last decision sounded good to Cassie too.

When they came to the stateroom door, Ruth turned to face her. "It's time to go."

"Yes."

Stepping forward, she hugged Cassie, briefly but fiercely. "No fuss, now!" With that she left, hurrying away as if Cassie might call her back if she didn't round the corner quickly enough.

But Cassie didn't call to her. She got it. Death really *was* putting out the lamp because the dawn had come.

IT WAS ALMOST EIGHT when Seamus felt Damen roll over, stretch, and leave the bed quietly, trying not to wake Christy. At least last night's encounter had gotten his host past the dread of sleeping in her dead sister's bed. In a short time, he heard the toilet flush and smiled to himself. Bathroom time with a host was something that took some getting used to, as Ronnie undoubtedly knew by now.

Christy woke despite Damen's efforts to be quiet, and Seamus heard her doubtful thoughts: *Was it too soon? Is he trying to get away before I wake up so he doesn't have to make excuses?* Her fears were relieved when Damen said gently from the doorway, "Do you like basketball?"

"I'm not sure."

"Well, if you're willing to give it a try, we could take in a Raptors game."

"I'm willing." Christy rose, pulled on a robe, and came to where he stood.

Damen kissed her tenderly. "I've got work tonight and some things to do before that. I have to go, but I—uh, you're something, Ms. Parker."

"You're okay too, Constable Damen."

As she followed him out of the room, Seamus began repeating "Paper. Yellow paper." She paused, and he repeated it again, slowly and clearly. "Yellow paper."

"John."

He stopped in the doorway, turning with an inquisitive expression.

"There was a piece of paper on the desk, and it's gone."

"What kind of paper?"

"It was a receipt for car repairs Henry Spellman ordered recently. I'd forgotten about it, but it just came to mind."

"Spellman?" He led her to the kitchen and pulled out a chair for Christy and another for himself. "Tell me about it. Tell me everything."

She explained about finding the receipt on the desk. "I didn't throw it away, so it should still be there, but it isn't."

"Who's been here?"

Christy's eyes widened. "Only Henry. He came by to pick up some things of his." Her voice turned angry as she remembered. "And he sent me on a wild goose chase through the apartment for a lighter that wasn't here! He must have taken the repair slip while I was looking in the hall closet."

"Imagine that paper," Damen ordered. "See if you can remember anything about it, the address of the shop or even the town."

"No, I don't think—"

John leaned toward her and repeated his request. "Think, Chris. What did it say?"

Christy shook her head. "I didn't pay much attention." Seamus whispered a word that she repeated aloud. "Lexus."

"What?"

"I think it said the repairs were made on a Lexus."

"That can't be right. Spellman drives a Camry."

"Oh." She shook her head. "I could be wrong. Albert was telling me the other night about his car, and I think that was a Lexus. Maybe I got them mixed up."

"Marle has a Lexus?"

"Yes. He keeps it at Henry's place, because he has this big garage—Ow!" She reacted as John grabbed her arm in a too-tight grip. "What?"

"I should have seen it! One of the men I interviewed mentioned Spellman's fancy car. He wasn't driving his Toyota, which is why it has no damage. They drove Marle's Lexus."

Christy put a hand to her mouth. "Wow. Kim must have really wanted to impress the home town crowd."

"Right." John was pacing now. "They took Albert's car, figuring he'd never know."

"But what if he knew the odometer reading? My dad always did."

"It's not that difficult to disable an odometer for a while." He massaged his neck absently. "So Spellman's in a real bind. He stole a car, he hit two people while driving drunk, and he left the scene. Now he's got to get the car fixed before Marle sees it."

"I bet he wasn't happy to hear you were coming to talk to them about the accident."

"Right." John rubbed his forehead impatiently. "I screwed up there too. One of the witnesses said the car was black. Spellman's car is a dark gray, but I thought she was mistaken. Witnesses are often mistaken about things like that."

"So no one knew the car wasn't Henry's?"

"Who up there would know Henry doesn't own a Lexus? The cars have similar body styles. They're both dark in color, and it was dark. Someone might have told us it wasn't a Camry if we'd asked, but we had no reason to think he wasn't driving his own vehicle."

"So Henry lied, hoping you'd take your investigation somewhere else," Christy said. "Once Albert's car is back in his garage, he'll be able to relax, especially now that he's got his receipt back."

Seamus was pleased with Christy's grasp of the situation but wondered how he might guide her to the next step. If Spellman was desperate to hide his crimes, then Cassie's death was very possibly murder.

Either Damen was a better-than-average policeman or Ronnie was working on her host, because he said to Christy, "Tell me again about Cassie's accident."

"She was backstage, and it was dark. A set piece came unhooked from its place and—" She stopped, her mouth still open. "You don't think—?"

"Maybe Spellman didn't want her to tell anyone about that repair order."

"You think he killed her?"

"We have to consider that possibility."

Christy pressed her lips together. "And Kim's helping him hide his crimes?"

"Has to be, though I'm not sure why she'd help him out. Intimidation, maybe."

Seamus could think of several other reasons. Kim wouldn't want to be associated with a scandal that might hurt her career. She'd wanted Henry Spellman for herself, and she certainly had him now. She might even hope to ride on his coattails to better parts or higher billing, a helping hand up the ladder from the troupe's leading man.

Damen checked his phone. "I'll get started on a search for the garage that has a Lexus in for repairs." He placed a quick kiss on her forehead. "I've got to go, but I'll be back as soon as I can."

"Tonight?" she asked. Blushing, she added, "You can stay here."

"*No!*" Seamus said firmly inside her head, and Damen winced as if he'd heard the same thing.

They both ignored the inner voices. "I'd like that." Looking at the floor and back to Christy, Damen said, "I want you to know I don't usually move this fast."

She stepped toward him, putting a hand on his arm. "I know. Me neither."

He seemed relieved to have said it aloud. "I've known since we were kids that you were the girl I wanted." He ran a hand through his short hair. "Sorry. Now I'm really moving too fast, but it's kind of a Catch-22. I don't want you to think I spend the night with every girl I meet, but I don't want you to run away in a panic screaming, "Stalker!" either. Weird, huh?"

She patted his face, smiling. "We can talk about it tonight."

"Yeah." He turned to go but looked back with a frown. "Be careful. If Spellman really did hit those people, and if he—" He stopped, unsure how to phrase it.

"—Hurt Cassie on purpose?" Christy shivered. "I can't believe that." Seamus felt her gulp to hold tears back. "We'll talk about it tonight. Maybe you'll know more by then."

Once Damen was out the door, she sank onto the couch, grief overcoming the happiness her night with John had created. Could it be that someone had actually wanted Cassie dead, someone her sister once thought she loved?

Christy had meant to go to the theatre early and get some work done, but she remained at the apartment, putting away the things she'd brought from Fairfield and thinking things over. Seamus felt her struggle to remain in control of her emotions. He felt sorry for her; she was not a person who'd ever thought she'd be involved with murder, and the thought that her sister might have been an innocent victim was almost too much to take.

She tried to restore a sense of normalcy by reading more of *Definitely Dickens.* It didn't help. The show was an ambitious undertaking, and she became even more distressed as she visualized the costumes still unfinished, some not even started. It was the biggest job she'd ever faced. And there was the matter of Tarcie's dress. What if her idea didn't work out?

Panic created a bubble in her chest that seemed likely to take over her whole body. Seamus, remembering how Christy's father had calmed her, said softly, "Parts." He didn't like to interfere with a host's thoughts unnecessarily, but this one had a lot to deal with. "Parts," he repeated.

The bubble began to dissipate, and Christy took a deep breath. "Parts," she said aloud. "One thing at a time."

Calmer, she showered, dressed, and headed to the subway station, determined to forget her doubts and fears. As she descended the stairs to the trains, Seamus noticed a figure waiting on the platform, swathed in more clothes than the sunny day required. Christy's glance passed right over the person, her glance so brief Seamus couldn't tell if the stranger was male or female. Christy faced the tracks, looking across at the other wall. It was frustrating to be unable to look where he wanted to look, and he tried a couple of times saying, "Back. Back." Absorbed in a poster about an upcoming concert at Roy Thompson Hall, she didn't respond.

Bothered by the figure he'd glimpsed, Seamus couldn't shake the feeling that Christy was in danger. He began again whispering, "Look. Look." She remained still, and he repeated, "Look!"

Several things happened at once. There was the sound of an approaching train. Footsteps echoed on the platform. And Christy finally obeyed his command, turning away from the gaping drop to see a figure rushing at her, arms outstretched.

It was a matter of inches. Because she turned, Christy's attacker succeeded only in bumping her roughly to the tiled floor as the train pulled up beside them. Seamus had no doubt she was meant to go over the edge, in front of the lead car which, even as it slowed to a stop, would have killed her. The figure hurried away, parting the crowd focused on Christy's fall and disappearing through it.

A woman down the platform came to help her up. "Are you all right?"

"Yes," Christy replied. "Someone bumped me, and I fell."

"I saw it," a man said. "It was a guy in one of those hoodie things."

"Drunk," the woman said. "Or high. You should report him to the TTC."

"Did you see what he looked like?" Christy turned to survey the platform. The faces crowded around her looked blank.

"Not really." The bell sounded, and the man backed away. "He had on a long gray coat over a hooded jacket. I didn't see his face."

Thanking the people who'd come to her aid, Christy assured them she was okay and hurried to get into a car before the train left the station. As she stood, holding the overhead bar for support, Seamus felt her legs begin to shake as the realization of what might have happened sunk in. At the first stop, a seat became available, and she almost fell into it. She was pretty certain she'd been pushed, not just jostled. *I'll tell John about it,* Seamus heard in her mind. *He'll know what to do.*

Christy said a little prayer of thanks to the guardian angel whose whispered warning saved her. *If I hadn't turned at the last moment, what would have happened?*

Inside her head, her not-an-angel, not-a-guardian smiled to himself. Even if such things weren't in his job description, he felt good about helping Christy escape a fate similar to her sister's.

Seamus intended to jump to Henry Spellman first thing, but again, it was not to be. Spellman wasn't at rehearsal, which irritated Albert Marle and frustrated Neen no end. "Doesn't he know we've got a show to get ready?"

"Kim's gone too," Marle said in disgust. "Odds are they're off somewhere together."

"Good grief! It isn't like they're fifteen years old."

Donna came along just then. "I can't find Josh, and it's past time to start."

Albert smacked his forehead in disgust. "He's the one who needs practice the most!"

"I'm here! I'm here!" Josh rushed in, his hair disheveled and his expression anxious. "I had some things to do this morning, and I ran a little late. Sorry."

He was met by cold stares from Albert, Donna, and even the usually genial Neen. Rather than explain further, Josh hurried to the stage, dumped his coat in a corner, and took his place with the rest of the dancers. "Humph!" Albert commented. "That young man's job is not first on his list of priorities."

"Yeah," Donna said grimly. "There's a lot of that going around."

Christy went upstairs, where three actors already waited for fittings. Donna, who'd followed her, glanced at her white face and told the actors, "Come back in five."

When they were gone she put an arm around Christy's shoulders. "Bad night, Sweetie?"

"Actually, it was wonderful."

"So what's wrong?"

"Oh, nothing," Christy lied, but her throat swelled again. "John and I got—you know, serious. Then I woke up this morning and remembered my sister is dead. I was—you know—and Cassie—"

Apparently Donna understood exactly what Christy was trying to say, and she hugged her tightly. "Sweetie, I know right now you think you should never enjoy anything again, but life is all about life." She leaned back to look at Christy's face. "Would Cass have wanted you to pass up a night with that hunky cop?"

Christy grinned weakly. "She always said I didn't have enough of a love life."

"Then you made your sister happy, wherever she is." Donna went into the bathroom at the back of the workshop, got some toilet paper, and handed it to Christy, who mopped her eyes and blew her nose. "Are you ready to take on gold lamé pants?" she asked. Glancing at eight neatly folded cut-outs ready to be sewn, she added, "I bet Dickens would roll over in his grave if he saw those things."

Laughing at her comment, Christy felt a sense of normalcy returning. Life really did go on, the good and the bad. She told Donna a light version of the incident in the subway, playing down the danger and relieving her own fear in the process. She'd forget about all the bad things and focus on making the day productive, she decided.

Glancing at the drawings on the corkboard wall, she took stock. Most of what was left to do was simple enough. There was only one item she was unsure about, and she thought today was the perfect day to tackle it. "Donna, I need to work on something else this morning. Will you tell everyone we'll get back to their fittings tomorrow?"

"Sure." Donna was obviously curious. "Does this have

anything to do with Tarcie?"

Christy smiled, though she was trembling on the inside. "I think I can work my way out of that particular corner, but only time will tell."

Knowing work would absorb Christy's mind, Seamus left with Donna and began moving through the cast and crew as opportunities arose. Hoping to find out more about Kim's weekend trip, he made his way to Amy, but what he learned wasn't helpful. She'd been unaware of the couple's destination, though she'd known they went somewhere together on their weekend off. The few details Kim had shared afterward related to Henry's sexual prowess. Amy had no idea they'd gone to Mason's Bridge or to a wedding reception, much less anything about a hit-and-run.

Amy knew Henry and Cassie had fought on the day Cassie returned to the Vic. Typically, Amy's reaction was filtered through self-interest, and she imagined how she'd have treated Cassie if she'd been Kim.

The rest of the company had nothing of interest to offer. Once Seamus got to Kim or Henry, he planned to stay until he learned something tangible. He'd felt guilt in both of them, it just hadn't been strong or deep. He should have paid more attention.

He jumped back to Donna when the cast assembled to rehearse the final number, a big production that would eventually include pinwheels, sparklers, and colorful banners. They practiced the steps and their various marks, learning who crossed where and when. Albert stood back, shouting commands, while Neen moved around, correcting an actor's stance or leading a line of dancers from Point A to Point B. It was a muddle, with frequent stops and starts as Albert cajoled and criticized.

"Marty, we want Victorian, not Lil-Rapper-Whoever. No pimp-walk. No strut."

"Suzi, when you raise your arms, don't block the face of the person behind you."

"Good! That segment looked almost like a dance number. Let's go over it again."

Neen came down the steps and stood with Albert as the music began again. "Is it ever going to come together?" he asked, optimism for once deserting him.

"A death, actors who decide on their own whether to show up for rehearsal, and a wardrobe mistress who's completely untried," Albert muttered. "It has to get better, because nothing else could go wrong."

Donna had joined them, her face damp with exertion from the demands of the dance. "Don't say things like that," she chided. "No matter what's happened already, things can always get worse."

Chapter Seventeen

"MIKE?"

He turned, and the smile that radiated peace settled on her. Cassie waited until he'd finished with a little boy who was trying to decide what kind of ice cream he wanted from a cart set up near the pool.

"There aren't a lot of good things about being dead," Mike told the child. "But ice cream anytime is one." The boy apparently agreed, because he took his cone and went happily off, licking twice for each step.

Mike watched him for a few seconds and then turned to Cassie. "How are you doing?"

"I can't remember things I should know."

He nodded. "It's distressing, but please believe me, it has to be this way."

She took a deep breath before speaking again. "I think I'm ready."

"Really."

She couldn't tell if he was displeased or not. "I know your guy is still back there, trying to find out if I died by accident, but I understand now. It doesn't matter."

Mike's smile deepened. "Well, actually, it matters until it doesn't."

She ignored the paradox. "Back there they talk about justice and punishment and fairness, but when you're dead—" She stopped, unable to find the right words.

"Cassie," Mike said. "If you're at peace, everything is as it should be."

"I was worried about my sister," she went on, explaining more to herself than to him, "but I can't change what happens to her. It won't help to know if she's coping or not coping. She's on her own."

Mike chuckled. "If your sister's anything like you, Cassie, I think she'll do well."

"I'm going to tell Nancy I'm ready." Touching his arm briefly in farewell, she turned to leave but then paused. "Will you thank Seamus for me?" she asked. "I'm grateful he was willing to help me, even if it wasn't necessary."

"You never know. He might do some good while he's there." Mike raised his hands in a comic gesture. "Life's funny, you know."

CHRISTY WAS PUTTING THE FINAL TOUCHES on her project when the ringtone she'd selected for John Damen, "Think of Me" from *Phantom*, sounded. "Hi," she said.

"How are things at the Vic?"

She'd changed her mind about telling him what happened on the subway. As she'd worked and the memory receded, she'd begun to question its importance. It really might have been an accident. Why make him worry?

He worried anyway. "I don't like you being in the same building with Spellman."

"He isn't here today. And why would he want to hurt me?"

"You saw the repair receipt. He could be afraid you'll make the connection too." She heard tension in his voice. "If I hadn't come asking questions, he'd think he was safe."

"John, it's your job to ask questions." Christy found it hard to believe in danger here in her domain. As they talked, she fiddled with the outfit displayed on a dressmaker's dummy. "Anything new on the hit-and-run?"

"Dad's calling every repair shop north of Toronto to find

out who fixed that car."

"Then it's just a matter of time until you prove Henry's guilty."

"But you need to be cautious until we get him locked up." She heard him sigh. "I wish I didn't have to work this afternoon."

"I'll be fine," Christy assured him. "I've got the whole company around me."

"Make sure you stay in a crowd of people," he ordered. "At least four at all times."

Looking around at the empty room, Christy smiled to herself. "I finished the job I was fretting over, so I can stay with the company for the rest of the day."

"I get off at midnight," John was saying. "Can you stay with them until I make it back there? I'd rather you didn't go home alone."

Christy considered. "I could go with the gang to Teddy's."

"Good. Wait for me there, and I'll pick you up."

She wondered if she should resent him giving her orders, but she didn't. It was possible Cassie had been murdered. It was possible someone had tried to hurt her in the subway. Though she was reluctant to believe it, John thought Henry

Spellman was a threat. Common sense told her that, despite her doubts, she should listen to him. Ornery cows on the farm she could handle. Potential killers were another story. "I'll wait at Teddy's," she promised. "See you when you get there."

Putting her phone away, Christy took a last look around before leaving the workroom. The parts were coming together, and according to the plan in her head, she'd get it done before full dress rehearsal. She'd even decided what the "unique" costume she'd promised Kim would look like, although she'd gone for simple elegance rather than making more work for herself. Glancing at the most important costume, the Dora Dress, she grimaced. She liked it, but her approval wasn't the issue. Still, she'd managed to take one part at a time, managed to handle the unexpected along with all her other jobs. She thought Dad would approve.

As she descended the stairs, the hum of activity pleased her. The cast was broken into groups, some going over difficult dance steps while others listened to Neen explain what the sets would look like and where the different pieces would be placed. Members of the set crew went about their tasks, ignoring the bustle around them.

Donna saw her coming, and her eyes asked a question. Christy nodded once to let her know she was ready. *I hope*, she added silently.

"Miss Parker!" Tarcie called as Christy's foot touched the last stair. "Is my costume ready to try on?" Her eyes bored into Christy's as if daring her to say either, "Yes," and have to prove it or, "No," and admit she wasn't keeping up with the demands of the job.

Christy kept her tone friendly. "Of course. When you're ready, I'll show you."

"That's good," Tarcie said sweetly, though her expression was about as sweet as vinegar. Turning, she said in a peremptory tone, "Albert, come upstairs. Miss Parker has something to show us."

Christy led the way, heart pumping. When her creation was revealed, she might be triumphant. Then again, she might be in trouble. No way to tell except to live through it.

At the doorway to the workroom, she stopped. "The dress isn't completely finished," she said, her hand on the doorknob. Tarcie almost purred with satisfaction. "It might need some adjustment at the hem, and maybe the neckline too."

With that she opened the door, a little dramatically, but she told herself the moment demanded it. In the center of the room was the dummy, draped in a dress different from Cassie's sketch but every bit the sumptuous gown Dora's character required. Its pale pink was a perfect choice for Tarcie's blond beauty, and it had all the additions and adornments high Victorian fashion required. Worn over a wide, hooped petticoat, the dress had several layers of skirting. Christy had opened the top layer in front and pulled it back to expose the creamy underskirt. Along the edges of the cut in the overskirt, she'd sewn a wide border of bright pink roses, which she'd matched along the hem of the under layer. After cutting off the tight, long sleeves the dress had originally had, she'd located a lacy shawl with a rose pattern perfectly matched to the varying shades of pink and tied it over the bodice as a fichu. The overall effect, a floating sea of roses, was dramatically Dickensian. There was no doubt that with a frilly parasol and fingerless gloves, the outfit would be perfect.

What Tarcie didn't know was that the dress came from Albert's collection. It was the one he'd reluctantly given up when Christy insisted pink wasn't his color.

Neither Albert nor Tarcie said anything for some time. They both looked shocked, though it was undoubtedly for different reasons. Christy waited breathlessly. Would Tarcie find something to hate about the dress? Would Albert blurt out that it had once belonged to him?

Tarcie apparently couldn't think of any criticism. "It's very good," she admitted.

Albert turned to Christy, eyes lit with amusement. "It's perfect." He cleared his throat before adding, "Try it on, Tarcie, and let Miss Parker make—" His eye twinkled. "—further adjustments. I should get downstairs before Josh breaks something."

Tarcie began unbuttoning the line of buttons that ran up the back of the dress, her expression betraying anticipation. When she'd retreated to the changing room, Albert said in a low voice, "It will look better on her than it ever did on me, Miss Parker." He leaned closer. "I thought Tarcie was up to something, but I think you've managed to come out of whatever it was very well."

"Just doing my job, Mr. Marle," Christy said. "Trying to make everyone look good."

THE EVENING PERFORMANCE WENT WELL, as any show should so late in its run. Everyone was present, which visibly relieved the tension in Neen's neck and shoulders. Christy avoided Kim and Henry, who, she heard from Donna, claimed they'd been sick from Thai food shared at dinner the evening before. Frustrated, Seamus jumped to Donna, then to Neen, and then to Marle, but none of them went anywhere near the two actors. Having already vented their anger, they punctuated it with avoidance.

Seamus stubbornly worked his way across the company. When he finally reached Spellman, he was immediately caught up in roiling emotions. Unlike the first time, Seamus found Henry fearful and guilt-ridden, struggling to push his disturbing thoughts aside in order to perform.

Kim squeezed Spellman's arm as he started onstage. "Keep it together, Henry." It was hard to tell if her words were meant as encouragement or warning. Spellman forced himself to become Charles Darnay, though his voice was thin and several times he had to be elbowed by other actors before remembering to speak his lines.

There was no thread to Spellman's thoughts, nothing

Seamus could follow. *Too much beer* came through at one point, but he pushed it away. In the middle of the second act his mind wandered again, and Seamus heard, *Cop suspects it was me.* After that Spellman steeled himself, mumbling softly, "Charles Darnay, Charles Darnay."

Seamus had to make a choice. Should he jump to Kim and learn what she knew or remain with Spellman? She had to have helped cover up the crime, but Kim's fierce anger allowed her to overcome her own guilt with the conviction that she could do no wrong. It seemed, however, that Henry was breaking down. His thoughts were more likely to reveal what Seamus needed to know. He decided to stay where he was and get back to Kim at rehearsals tomorrow.

Chapter Eighteen

CHRISTY DID AS SHE'D PROMISED, remaining with the cast and crew. When the show ended, she asked Josh and Randy if they planned to stop at Teddy's for a drink. Josh chuckled. "Don't we always?"

"Do you mind if I tag along? I'm meeting someone there."

"That dreamy cop, I suppose?" Randy rolled his eyes. "How'd you hook up with that?"

Because Christy liked the boys, she answered honestly. "He's an old friend. And how does everyone know he's a cop?"

Randy gave her a wicked smile. "Rumors, girlfriend. Everyone's interested."

While Josh searched for the spot where he'd dropped his coat earlier ("Never in a logical place," Randy complained), Christy waited by the door, saying goodnight to the company as they passed. When they finally came along, Josh apologized for taking so long. "Her Highness deigned to speak to me," he said, making a comic face. "Watch out, Christy. I think Kim's interested in your hunky policeman."

"You're kidding!" Randy put his hands on his hips in a gesture of disgust and turned to Christy with a gossipy air. "We've seen cracks in the Henry/Kim collaboration today."

"Already!" Josh added.

"She's after Christy's guy?" Randy asked. "She wants to steal another girl's property?"

"She asked if Christy and he are an item."

"And what did you tell her?" Randy clearly didn't think Kim's nosiness deserved satisfaction.

Josh seemed slightly cowed. "I told her they were meeting at Teddy's later."

"You are a cretin. Now she'll show up and do her distressing version of temptress." Randy put a hand on Christy's arm. "I swear, it would make you sick."

"No worries," Josh said. "She and Henry have reservations somewhere downtown." He smacked the back of Randy's head. "And I am not a cretin, you imbecile."

"You are so, and a secretive one at that." Randy turned serious, and Christy sensed trouble. "You were late for rehearsal again today, for about the fourth time. That's not to mention the two you missed entirely. Isn't it time you told me where you've been sneaking off to?"

There was a long silence, and Christy realized with dismay that Randy had purposely chosen to confront Josh when she was present, fearing the answer.

Josh looked around to assure there was no one else nearby. "If you must know, I'm taking dance lessons."

"Dance lessons?" Christy and Randy spoke in chorus.

He raised his palms and shoulders in a comic gesture of concession. "I lied on my app, okay? Said I'd had all this training, when all I had was the director at my high school hollering, "Step, kick, three, four," over and over until I got it into my head. The new show calls for way more dance moves than I've got."

"But you've *been* dancing," Randy said. "We've been practicing for weeks."

"I've been doing what you do, and you know Neen's been on my case about it," Josh chewed a nail briefly and then put the hand behind his back with a firm effort. "I'm always half a step behind, because I have to look at what you're doing and copy it."

"Great boogley-woogley," Randy said, unable to come up

with something coherent.

"I take private lessons from an old guy who lives near you, Chris. It's where I was going the day you saw me on the street." Josh rolled his eyes. "He's good, but he's a temperamental old thing. If I don't get it right, I have to stay till I do. That's why I've been late and even missed a few rehearsals."

"You didn't think I'd help you?" Randy asked, hurt in his voice.

"I was embarrassed to tell you how little I know. I have to study the terminology just to keep up with you." Josh slipped into his coat. "This guy helps with execution: where my hands go, what to do with my head, all the stuff you learned when you were nine."

"Seven," Randy corrected absently. "I just can't believe you didn't tell me."

"Don't be mad, Ran," Josh begged. "If we're ever going to move up, I have to get better. A Vic revue is one thing, but someday we'll do *42ⁿᵈ Street* on Broadway, right?"

Randy was tempted to pout, but good nature won out. "Actually, I'd prefer *A Chorus Line*, but yeah, I guess we both need to work harder." The air cleared, and Christy relaxed a little. They left the theatre with the boys on either side of her, peace restored.

It was three blocks to the bar, and they found themselves skidding on the icy street. The two men held Christy's elbows to stabilize her, but they all struggled to stay upright. They maintained their footing through group effort, and all three were laughing by the time they reached Teddy's.

Inside, it was warm and dark, and the sounds of conversation, '80s music, and tinkling glasses met their ears. They ordered drinks and took them to a table in the corner. Soon they were joined by others from the cast, and time passed quickly as they chatted about the current show and how well the new one was coming together.

Christy relaxed, enjoying the company of her friends. There was no sign of Henry Spellman, and John would be on his way soon. Time passed quickly.

Josh and Randy sat with Christy for a while, but eventually one and then the other moved off to speak with other actors from the Vic who'd stopped by. It didn't matter; people came and went steadily, some interested in what their costumes would look like, others just chatting about generalities.

The chairs on either side of her were unoccupied briefly, and she sipped her drink, watching Randy at the bar, telling a story that entailed a lot of gesturing. Someone slipped in beside her, and she turned to find Tarcie, a drink in her hand and a tentative smile on her face.

"Miss Parker."

"Please, I'm Christy to everyone here."

Tarcie looked down at her hands. "I wasn't sure if we were friends or not."

Christy tried to keep her right eyebrow from rising, as she'd been told it did when she was surprised. *Friends?*

"I might owe you an apology," Tarcie said. Her lips were stiff, as if it was hard to speak the words.

"No—" Christy began, but Tarcie raised a hand.

"I can be overbearing, and I sometimes make assumptions I should not."

Christy was beginning to be embarrassed. Why was the company's lead actress apologizing to her? "Really, it was nothing," she managed before Tarcie went on.

"I thought my uncle was being...reckless, inviting you to see his...collection. You were new to the group, and I was afraid you would...share the information with others. I'm sure you can see that it's best if very few people know of his...interest."

"Of course." She didn't elaborate. Tarcie wasn't going to get any details out of her, if that's what she was after.

Tarcie played with the ring of moisture her glass had left on the table. "I don't mean to stick my nose into Albert's business."

So many people said that when it was exactly what they did!

"My uncle has worked very hard to make the Vic a reputable theatre company in this city. He's done a fine job." Tarcie bit her lip. "I'd hate it if he became a laughingstock." Christy was surprised to see real emotion in Tarcie's eyes. "The drag queen at the Vic. It would be awful!"

Christy was just beginning to feel sorry for Tarcie when the selfish part came out. "He has no family except me, at least not anyone who'd be interested in taking over the Vic when he retires. If he could just be discreet, I'd actually have something worthwhile to do when I'm too old to play leads."

The feeling of empathy dissipated. "He sent you to apologize, didn't he?"

Tarcie lifted her chin. "He didn't send me. He suggested

I've been less than welcoming, and if I'm ever going to manage a large group, I have to become less—" She hesitated before using the word Albert had apparently used, "—bitchy."

Christy took a sip of beer to hide a smile. Dear Albert! "I appreciate your letting me know," she told Tarcie. Thoughts of Albert's collection brought another smile. "And I'm glad you like your Dora dress."

A while later, she was talking with Beverly when Josh appeared at her elbow, his expression somewhat amused, somewhat irritated. "I think we're going to take off," he told her. "Randy needs to get home."

"No, I don't," Randy responded, coming up behind them and draping an arm around their necks. "Don't listen to Josh. He's a poop." He giggled. "I mean a pooper." With one more try, he got it right. "A party pooper."

"Randy doesn't drink," Josh explained to Christy. "Except for tonight, apparently."

"I only had two," Randy said, putting up three fingers. "Two."

Josh ignored him. "I hate to leave you here alone, but you see how he is." Randy snapped his fingers to get the barmaid's attention. "He'll be barfing soon. No tolerance."

Christy gave him a playful shove. "Go, Josh! I'm hardly alone, and John will be here soon. I'll be fine."

"Are you sure? When you asked to come with us, I thought you might have a reason. Is somebody bothering you?"

Glancing around the room, she assured herself that Spellman wasn't present. "Nobody here scares me, Josh. Now get Randy home before he embarrasses himself."

HENRY SPELLMAN left the theatre after putting Charles Darnay away for the night. Inside his head, Seamus tried to pick up specifics about the weekend in Mason's Bridge, the breakup with Cassie, and the repairs on Albert's car. It wasn't possible, because Spellman kept burying it. He got only a general sense of undefined but crushing guilt.

As Spellman exited the front entrance, hoping—and Seamus guessed this was unusual—there were no fans hanging around, he glimpsed Kim a block ahead. Spellman was surprised she hadn't waited for him. *God knows she's been under my elbow for the past week.*

Kim carried a tote bag, and she was in a hurry. Seamus was gratified to pick up a flash of resentment from his host. In Spellman's mind Kim's pouty face appeared and her pleading voice sounded. *Hank, my sister's getting married this weekend, and my Mom keeps making comments about how odd it is her oldest daughter isn't married yet.*

When he'd murmured something sympathetic, she'd made her point. *I have to go, but I can't show up without a date. A stud."* She'd added with a smile of promise, *Cassie never has to know, and I'll pay for everything."* Leaning in so he got a look down her blouse, she'd said, *I'd be really grateful, Hank.*

"So sweet then," Spellman muttered bitterly. "Now she scuttles away like a mouse looking for a place to hide."

A lovers' quarrel? Seamus wondered. Maybe Kim was beginning to regret helping Spellman cover up the hit-and-run.

Henry started after her as if he'd made a decision. He remained some distance back, even when Kim stopped outside Teddy's Bar. Instead of going in, she took up a spot across the street from the entrance. Spellman stepped into the shadows of an alley, his thoughts unsettled. *What is she up to?* Whatever it was, he didn't like it.

It was cold, and as Spellman tried to concentrate on something besides his rapidly chilling feet, Seamus learned some things. First, Spellman had cared for Cassie, at least as much as someone as self-centered as he could care for another person. Second, he'd realized almost as soon as she hurried off wearing his jacket that the receipt for car repairs was in the pocket. He'd been frantic to think that his angry ex-girlfriend possessed information that could get him into trouble.

Taking Albert's car had been Kim's idea, and again, she'd used her charm to get him to agree. *Wouldn't it be fun to take the Lexus, Hank? We'll have it back tomorrow, and Albert will never know. I know how to unhook the odometer. I did it lots of times to my parents' car when I was younger.*

The way she'd proposed it, and the way she'd touched his arm, his face, even his thigh, had scrambled Henry's thoughts, and he'd agreed without considering the consequences if something went wrong. And something had gone terribly wrong.

It came as a surprise to Seamus that Spellman had

thought until recently he'd hit a deer. That explained his lack of deep guilt earlier. His concern then had been covering up the damage to Albert's car. Damen's visit had changed things, and now Henry was more agitated, much less stable.

It was an accident, he told himself. *I had too much to drink. I'm not responsible.*

"Being drunk isn't an excuse." Seamus yielded to an angry impulse before he could stop himself.

"Ahhh!" Spellman jumped as if he'd been branded, and Seamus reminded himself it wasn't good to startle a host. Despite his objections to Spellman's pathetic excuses, he had to maintain control.

With an unsettled mind and the cold sidewalk underfoot, Spellman finally grew tired of waiting. *Got to get to Christy.* As he left his hiding place, Seamus was struck with dread. It was almost midnight, and many people from the Vic had already left the bar, heading for the subway, the bus, or walking toward home. Damen hadn't yet arrived.

Turning away from the bar, Spellman made his way down a few blocks, where he crossed the street, keeping to the shadows so Kim wouldn't see him. Seamus tried to figure out what he intended, but there didn't seem to be a coherent plan. The incident in the subway suggested Christy was in danger, but Spellman was apparently acting purely on instinct.

Continuing down the cross street to an alley that cut the block in half, Spellman hurried along until he came to the back of the bar. There was a fence with a gate, which he entered, crossing a courtyard meant for outside dining in summer. Snow-draped and dark, with metal tables and chairs stacked under a tarp in one corner, it looked gloomy and unwelcoming. Spellman went through the back door, down a short hallway that passed the kitchen and the rest rooms, and entered the bar.

Christy sat by herself at a table, one of only three customers left in the place. The other two, leaning their elbows on the long, highly polished bar, looked to be late-night, long-term drinkers. Christy's phone lay on the table before her, a half-finished glass of beer beside it. Looking at the phone, she didn't notice Spellman until he spoke.

"Christy."

When she looked up and recognized him, Seamus saw that she was afraid. She glanced at the bar, where a skinny barmaid was all the authority the place offered. Seamus saw her pull courage from somewhere inside herself and put it on like a cloak. "Hello, Henry," she said calmly.

Seamus jumped to Christy, knowing he had little sway over Spellman if his intent was murderous. He hoped to help her in some way, though he wasn't sure how.

Aware of the danger she faced, she was unwilling to succumb to panic. Suppressing the wave of nausea that was partly Seamus' fault, she said casually, "Have a seat. Everyone else has gone home."

"Are you waiting for someone?"

"I am."

"That cop, maybe?"

Her eyes met his steadily. "Yes."

Just then the phone sounded the snippet of "Think of Me." Christy smiled apologetically and took the call. Seamus heard what Christy heard, though Spellman got a different message.

"Hello."

"Christy, I'm sorry I'm late. We had an accident that turned into a standoff with a drunk driver."

"Yes, I have been waiting a while."

"I'm going to be a bit longer, but I should get there before closing. Are you all right?"

"Great," Christy replied. "Ten minutes would be great."

There was a pause. "It'll be longer than that. I have to take statements and I need—"

"I get it. Ten minutes. I'll be here." She sounded gently exasperated with him.

Another pause, and Damen's voice changed. "You're in trouble."

Christy smiled at Spellman and lowered her eyes as if embarrassed. "Of course, silly."

"I'm coming." His voice was tense. "No matter what, stay where you are."

"I will. Bye." She set the phone aside. "He was delayed, but he'll be here shortly."

Spellman seemed unsure what to do. "That's good," he said weakly. "I just thought you might be uncomfortable, sitting here alone."

"I'm fine," she said, "You go home and get some sleep, Henry. You look tired."

CHRISTY'S SIGH OF RELIEF when Spellman left was so loud that one of the denizens at the bar turned to look. She managed a smile, and the man turned back to his drink and the hockey game without responding. As adrenalin faded in her blood, the fight or flight urge faded too. John would arrive soon.

"Miss Parker." The voice at her elbow was almost a whisper. "I've got a gun, so do as I say. We're going to leave together, like old friends. You'll say nothing to anyone. Got it?"

Turning her head a little, Christy saw Kim Snyder's stony face. The press of a metal object at her ribcage attested to the seriousness of the threat. Even as fear chilled her blood, she had a moment of disgust that she'd missed it. Henry was weak, as the woman at the Vic had said. He hadn't coerced Kim into keeping quiet, and she was no frightened witness to his crime. She was an active accomplice.

Christy's next thought was to call for help, but logic told her it would do her no good. Kim could kill her with a twitch of a finger and might even kill the others in the bar. There was nothing to do but obey and hope for a chance to escape once they got outside. John was on his way. The barmaid would tell him she'd left with Kim. Would he arrive in time to save her from being killed?

She rose from the bench, taking her coat off the hook and putting it on as slowly as possible. How might she save herself? When she turned to Kim, she glimpsed a small pistol, covered by a scarf that complemented her fashionable coat. She wasn't sure if it was worse to see it or to feel it against her side. It was deadly either way.

When she'd delayed as long as she could, Christy turned toward the front door, but Kim ordered, "We'll go out the back." As they left, Kim giggled and leaned on Christy, feigning drunkenness which allowed her to keep the gun pressed to her captive's side. Kim was no doubt setting up her story for later: she'd left with Christy but went home, having had too much to drink.

Once they were outside, Kim gave up her staggering performance, letting go of Christy's arm as if repelled by the need to touch her. "Hand over your phone." Christy did as ordered, and Kim tossed it into a snow bank.

"You killed my sister." Anger was replacing Christy's fear, at least some of it.

Kim's face was pale in the dimness, but Christy saw her

casual smile. "I didn't intend to kill her, if that helps. I needed to get her away from the Vic when your boyfriend the cop came with his questions." Kim gestured slightly with the gun. "I hid Amy's vest, knowing she'd whine to Cassie, which she did. Cassie, being the good little helper, volunteered to come in early the next day to look for it."

"And you were there. You unhooked the guillotine and let it hit her as she passed."

"As I said, it wasn't supposed to be a death blow. All I wanted was for her to be away from the theatre when Damen came by." Kim's tone resolved herself of all responsibility for the murder of another human being.

"And this was all because Cass knew Albert's car was in the repair shop?"

There was a pause. "I suppose your boyfriend knows it was Albert's car we took, if you do." She pressed the heel of her free hand to her head as if it hurt. "Damn it! Once I got Cassie out of the way, I thought we'd be all right. Why did you stick around instead of going back to your little hick town where you belong?"

A voice behind Christy surprised them both. "You killed Cassie?"

"Henry!" Kim took a step back. "What are you doing here?"

"Did you kill Cassie?" The words came slowly, as if he had to force each one separately.

Kim recovered her poise. "If you were eavesdropping, you know it was an accident."

"And what about Christy? Is she going to have an accident too?" His eyes widened as a thought came to him. "Someone said she almost fell onto the subway track this morning. Is that where you got those bruises?"

"I hit the turnstile pretty hard," Kim admitted. "Thought I broke something."

Henry seemed stunned. "That's why you weren't home when I stopped. You were out trying to kill Christy."

"Henry, she saw the receipt. She knows what her sister knew."

"They won't believe another accident," Christy said. "John won't believe it."

"Then it'll be suicide," Kim said, her voice matter-of-fact. "You recently lost your dad and your sister, the new job put you under pressure, and you just couldn't take it." She chewed her bottom lip thoughtfully. "I'll call Donna first thing in the morning. I'll tell her we talked after the show and I'm worried about your mental state."

"Kim, you can't do this." Spellman stood up straighter, as he did just before going onstage, and his voice took on an authoritative note. "I won't let you."

There was a pause as she thought about that. "What are you going to do, Henry?"

"I'll tell the police everything, how you wanted to sneak into your parents' house and have sex in your old bedroom." He put his hands up to his face. "I don't even remember driving there! I never saw those people in the road!" His voice rose to a sob. "I didn't mean it. I was drunk."

"News flash, Hank. You weren't driving."

The shot was so loud that Christy thought for a second the building beside them had exploded. Spellman let out a groan and dropped to his knees. He wavered briefly before falling forward, making no attempt to save his face from the impact. In a spill of light from a security lamp, Christy saw a dark stain spread across his coat as he lay motionless in the dirty alley.

"Let's go. Someone's likely to report the shot." Kim gave Christy a push with the barrel of the gun. Having proof of her willingness to use it, Christy obeyed without delay, her mind a whirl of fear. Kim directed her down the alley, where street lights didn't penetrate and the pavement was slippery with snow, ice, and garbage. Once she turned to look back at Henry. Nothing moved. No one came to investigate the single gunshot. Perhaps the police would be called, but by the time they arrived, where would she be? And in what condition: dead, or alive?

Kim's view of Christy's immediate future soon became evident. "Let's go back to the Vic, where we can get this done right."

Chapter Nineteen

Seamus' mind raced as Kim hurried Christy along, repeatedly jabbing her in the side with the gun. Kim muttered, half to herself, "Okay, this works. You shot Henry, who betrayed your sister. Add it to your reasons for suicide. He can take the blame for stealing Albert's car and hitting those people. I can be the one who was passed out in the back seat. I never knew what happened. I'll be absolutely horrified. It works. It really works."

Christy said what Seamus was thinking. "You can't keep getting away with murder."

"I told you! I did not murder your sister!" The last word came out in a hiss.

"You didn't help those people. The woman died, and the man might have."

"They were in the road." She tossed her head angrily. "It was their own fault."

Christy didn't argue, a decision Seamus approved. No

way would she convince Kim she was wrong.

As they approached the theatre, Christy looked up at the third-story windows. They were dark. Albert was either asleep or away. Guessing her thought, Kim sneered, "Our illustrious leader's probably zoned out on pills and wine."

Propelled by terse commands, Christy entered the alley alongside the building. It was dark and slippery, and she found it difficult to stay upright. Hearing Kim grunt a couple of times as she also struggled with her footing, Seamus nursed a hope that she'd trip and fall. If she did, should he encourage Christy to run? No. He recalled Josh, or maybe it was Randy, mentioning that Kim was an excellent shot. Where could Christy go in the narrow alley to escape a bullet?

The thought led to a truth he had to consider. If Christy died here tonight, he had to jump to someone else, or he'd be unable to return to the ship. Ever. It was something every cross-back had to face, the possibility he might be stranded on earth, a lost soul. Seamus pushed the thought to the back of his mind. *Worry about that later.* If he could keep Christy alive, the question of jumping would be moot.

When they'd stumbled their way to the back entrance,

Kim ordered, "I know you have a key, so use it." Obediently Christy took the key from her purse and opened the door. As they entered the dark building, Kim took hold of Christy's collar to stop her while she turned the deadbolt. "Now," she ordered, "up the stairs to your little wardrobe world."

As Christy made her way up the stairs, Seamus considered the options. Kim would be reluctant to fire the gun with Albert in the building. Even if he were asleep, a shot would get his attention. Poison was a possibility, but he doubted Kim had the time or the know-how to arrange such a death.

As he tried to guess Kim's plan, he fought a sense of despair within himself. A lot of this was his fault. He'd missed the signs that it was Kim, not Spellman, who was capable of murder. Now Christy might die because of it. "Talk," he ordered, hoping Christy could slow Kim down with conversation and keep her from thinking.

"Talk," he said again.

Christy said, "Was it you up here that first day?"

"What?" Kim was obviously distracted. "Oh. Yes. I was hoping Cassie'd left that stupid work order in the wardrobe room. I crawled through the transom to look for it, but it wasn't there. Then you and Donna showed up and I had to hide." They reached the costume room and she ordered, "Unlock the door."

Inside the workroom, Kim turned on the lights. "Nobody to see us back here," she said briskly. Twisting her head toward the dressing room at the back, she ordered, "You'll need to wait in there till I get things ready." As Christy passed, Kim snatched the keys from her hand. "I'll return these after you succumb to grief and the knowledge of your own deficiency."

Seamus jumped to Kim before she closed the door. He was no help to Christy if they were both locked in a four-by-four cell.

Inside Kim's head, Seamus was again struck by the intensity of the woman's anger. She'd been confident that her role in the hit-and-run wouldn't be discovered, and she was furious the problem had arisen again. She muttered aloud as she pulled a chair up to the door of Christy's prison, "This works. It'll all settle down once you're gone." She set the back of the chair under the knob and wedged it tightly, adding, "They shouldn't have hired you anyway. An amateur, for god's sake! Stupid Albert!"

Seamus could discern no remorse in Kim Snyder: not for the accident that left one dead and one barely alive; not for Henry Spellman, her lover; not for Cassie Parker; and certainly not for Christy, whose death was simply another item on Kim's to-do list.

"Light. I need a light." After a short search, Kim located a flashlight on a shelf near the worktable. The notebook lay open on the top, causing another wave of irritation. "A lot of good it did me to steal the notes on Tarcie's costume." She spoke in Christy's direction, though Seamus doubted the girl could hear. "I thought she'd lay down the law with Uncle Al and get you fired, but you got out of it somehow, didn't you?"

Kim left the wardrobe room, locking the door with Christy's key. Using the flashlight, she located a pair of cotton gloves in one of the crates along the back wall. After pulling them on, she went quietly down the stairs and rummaged in the crew's storage area until she found a length of sturdy rope. Back upstairs, she tied one end of it to the banister that ran along the loft edge. After testing the knot's strength with a few pulls, she dropped the other end over the rail, realized it came too close to the floor below, and pulled it up again. Untying the knot, she re-tied it so the end hung about ten feet off the stage floor. Pulling the free end up again, she made a slipknot and tested the resulting noose to be sure it slid freely open and closed. "That works," she said with satisfaction. Not only was Seamus tired of hearing that phrase, he was afraid she might be correct.

Next Kim went back to the crates and directed her light on them until she located one labeled *Scarves*. Bringing the whole crate out to the railing, she sorted through for one that suited her purpose. "No sense in you seeing what's coming," she muttered in Christy's general direction. "We should probably tie your hands too, so you can't fight me." She took a second scarf, tested its strength, and kicked the box aside.

Although Kim's mind wasn't easy to read, Seamus got it. She intended to blindfold Christy and lead her to the railing. Disoriented and unable to see where she was, Christy would be defenseless. Kim would slip the rope over her head and shove her over the rail before she understood what was happening. In the morning someone would find her, apparently dead by her own hand. He guessed the gun that killed Henry would be wiped clean of prints and hidden in the sewing area somewhere.

It was time to interfere. Summoning all his strength, Seamus inflated himself as much as possible inside Kim's head. With all his energy he flailed and rattled, shouting, "No!" over and over.

He failed. Kim wasn't the type of person to be turned from her intent by an inner voice some would interpret as conscience. If anything, she became angrier and more convinced that once Christy Parker was dead, quiet would return to her mind.

When she'd arranged everything the way she wanted it, Kim went to retrieve Christy from her prison. Seamus made a fuss again, redoubling his efforts and causing as much disturbance in her mind as he could manage. It had only a slight effect. Kim stopped for a second, one hand on her stomach as she reeled from the unfamiliar sensations. But a cross-back couldn't stop a determined host, and she soon re-took control. With a gulp to quell her nausea and a frown of concentration, Kim entered the workroom, went to the dressing closet, took the chair from under the doorknob, and opened the door.

At least, she tried to. The handle turned only slightly, and the door wouldn't open. Christy had clicked the privacy lock on the inside. Snarling in irritation, Kim rattled the knob. "Open this door! Open it!" she ordered. There was no response.

Calming herself with effort, Kim tried a different tactic. "I'm not going to hurt you, Christy. I've decided I don't need to. All I'm going to do is lock you in the basement."

No answer. Kim tried again. "It'll take them a while to find you, and by then I'll be long gone. For you, it will only mean a few hours in the dark."

Still no response. Kim spoke louder. "Do you hear me, Christy? I won't hurt you." She wasn't a very good actress, Seamus decided, for her voice sounded as fake as the old ladies who tell small children that Santa won't stop at their homes if they're naughty. The lie apparently fell on deaf ears, and it remained quiet on the other side of the door.

Kim grabbed the doorknob and rattled it a couple of times. "If I have to shoot you through this door, I will, Christy! You don't have to die if you'll just cooperate."

Still no reply. Seamus wondered what Christy had planned, but he was washed in a wave of fury as Kim lost her temper completely. Rattling the handle wildly, she thumped her shoulder against the door and pulled on the knob with mighty effort. Every few seconds she kicked the wood in pure frustration then went back to jerking the handle like a madwoman.

Precisely timed between Kim's pushing and pulling, something clicked on the other side, and the door flew open. Off balance, Kim staggered backward, her grasp on the doorknob all that kept her from falling to the floor.

Christy rushed at her, holding a short wooden stool. Using it as a club, she whacked Kim soundly on her right shoulder. Yelping in pain, Kim went down on one knee, putting her hands out to stop herself from falling onto her rear.

Throwing the stool at her, Christy ran from the room, switching off the light as she passed and closing the door behind her before her dazed enemy could recover. Seamus himself was so surprised at the bold move that he failed to jump to her as she passed. Probably best, he told himself as Kim got to her feet and began groping for the gun. Christy would need all her strength to get out of the theatre alive. His best move was to continue interfering with Kim's intentions whenever possible.

John Damen's reaction to Christy's call for help was immediate and somewhat dangerous. Ronnie was aware that she couldn't die a second time, but she also knew if Damen killed himself trying to get to Christy, she'd be unable to return to the ship. Thinking of that, and of the need for her host to live until he could rescue the woman he loved, she counseled caution as Damen careened through the streets like a madman.

Despite his alarming speed, John divided his time between calling Christy and calling for help. There was no answer from Christy. A call to police in the 22nd Division resulted in a return call minutes later. She was no longer at Teddy's. "Did she leave with a man?"

After a moment the patrolman replied, "The bartender says she left with one of the actresses from the Vic."

Damen began recalculating his route. "Can you guys check out her apartment?" he asked the cop. "I'm fifteen minutes out. You're a lot closer."

He heard a huff of disapproval, and the man's voice

changed. "You said this woman was in danger, that some guy was going to kill her, but she left Teddy's with a friend from work. Now you want us to go to her house?"

"I don't know what's going on, but she sent me an S.O.S."

"What'd she say?"

"That I should be there in ten minutes, but she knew I can't do that. She needs help."

There was a pause as the officer talked to someone else. "Look, Damen. Just because you're a cop doesn't mean we can keep tabs on your girlfriend for you. She was sitting at a table with her phone in front of her. Her friend came in and they left together, maybe a little bit drunk. She took her phone with her. She could have called if she needed help."

With a groan of frustration, Damen hung up and pressed the accelerator a little harder. Ronnie's only hope was that when her host wrapped his car around a light pole, there'd be someone close she could jump to before he breathed his last.

IF KIM SNYDER HAD BEEN ANGRY BEFORE, she was livid now. After locating her gun and the flashlight, she threw open the door of the workroom, scanning the dark loft for a sign of her quarry. Seamus longed to know where Christy was too but hoped he didn't see her through Kim's eyes.

As Kim listened to the darkness, he heard Ronnie's voice. "Seamus! Where are you?" Kim's whole body stiffened at the sound, unintelligible to her but still audible. He answered, "Theatre."

That Kim understood. "Theatre?" she echoed. Predictably, her response was anger. Seamus felt the force of it, pushing against him, limiting him. She was almost mad with it. He would have to back off, at least for a while. Kim's emotional upheaval might block his ability to communicate with Ronnie.

"I'll try." Ronnie's response indicated Damen was absorbed in something, probably driving, and she didn't want to distract him. Seamus knew she'd begin planting the idea of the Vic in his mind. Now if Christy could stay alive until he arrived.

There'd been no sound from the metal stairway, which vibrated when someone hurried up or down the steps. "She's up here somewhere," Kim murmured.

Seamus agreed. Not only were the stairs noisy, the open

framework with its turn halfway down would offer Christy to Kim as a clear target. Worse, the EXIT sign below lit the bottom section of stairs, and the locked exit door would take time to navigate, time Christy wouldn't have with Kim standing above her with a gun.

Kim moved slowly toward the racks of costumes. At the end of each, she bent and shone the light along the bottom, looking for Christy's huddled form, or at least her feet. At each row she found nothing. Past the racks was the back wall and a small storage closet. Pulling the door open with a jerk, she shone her light inside. Only assorted props and unused sound equipment lay revealed in the light. Seamus caught the scent of dust burned onto electronic devices. Closing the door, Kim turned back, listening for movement. Nothing.

Keeping the light focused forward, she walked slowly to the stairway, stopping to listen after each step. There was no sound except her breathing. "Gone," Seamus whispered. "Gone, gone."

An odd noise sounded nearby, and Kim stopped, trying to decide what it was. The rhythmic scrape continued, something rubbing against metal, like—like a rope against a wrought-iron banister. When Seamus realized what it was, he again made a fuss, trying to distract Kim. It didn't take her long, however, to realize that Christy was using the rope arranged for her hanging as an escape route.

Kim hurried to the railing, shining her light downward. The beam caught Christy just as she reached the end of the rope. Still several feet above the floor, she let go, breaking her fall by grabbing the cyclorama with one hand. Kim fired a shot, but Christy was already gone, scrambling down the curtain and rolling under it and onto the stage.

A moment later, a door opened at the far end of the theatre. Lit from behind, Albert Marle stood in the balcony doorway, peering into the darkness. "Who's down there?"

"Get back," Christy shouted from the shadows. "She's got a gun!"

A second shot rang out. Marle ducked out of the lighted doorway, though the shot was aimed at the sound of Christy's voice and not at him.

After a few seconds he called out, "Whoever's down there, I'm locking myself in my apartment and calling the police. I suggest you leave." Noises followed, possibly the sound of someone alligator-crawling along the wooden floor. The lighted rectangle disappeared as the door slammed shut. Silence reigned in the dark theatre, but Seamus heard Kim mutter to herself, "If I kill her before the cops arrive, there's not one thing to prove I was here tonight."

Chapter Twenty

Damen pulled up at the Vic, stopping so abruptly that Ronnie wondered if someone with no body could still get whiplash. Exiting the car at a run, he approached the doors. He peered between the metal burglar bars and through the glass, seeing only darkness inside. As he began to doubt himself, or rather, to doubt the whispers Ronnie'd been repeating, he heard a voice, a living one this time, from above. "Are you the police?"

Looking up, Ronnie saw a three-quarter-sized Ebenezer Scrooge, complete with dressing gown, leaning out the window as if looking for a boy to run and buy him a Christmas goose. Damen recognized the man, though a name didn't come to mind. "I'm looking for Christy Parker."

"They all left hours ago," the man said, "but there's a prowler. I called the police."

"Can you let me in?" Damen asked. "I think Christy's in there, and she's in trouble."

"I've locked myself in, but—" His face twisted in thought. "There's a back door down the alley. It might be how they got in."

Damen was gone before he'd finished the sentence. As he made his way, slipping and almost falling in his hurry, Ronnie called out, "Seamus! Help's on the way." Damen reeled for a moment at the noise in his head, but he didn't hesitate, determination foremost in his mind.

The door was locked. Damen struck it with his fist in frustration. "Damn!"

Ronnie was almost as upset as he. "Seamus! Seamus, the door's locked."

After a moment, his voice came to her, faint but discernible. "Fire escape. Out back."

"Back." Ronnie said to Damen, softly but clearly. "Back."

He didn't get it for a while and stood slumped against the door, trying to decide what to do. With his head in the mess it was, Ronnie gave Damen credit for not succumbing to panic. "Back," she repeated. "Back."

Finally he responded, pushing away from the metal door and heading to the back of the building. When he got there, Ronnie changed her message. "Up," she ordered. "Up."

Damen looked up. Above his head was a metal fire escape, its lowest extension stored against the railing of the first-floor landing. Seeing the window beside it, he didn't need Ronnie's last, "Up!" to know what to do. He began jumping, reaching for the ladder.

The ice helped, raising him a few inches so he finally caught hold of the ladder's bottom rung. Swinging his body back and forth a few times, Damen got his feet onto the base of the fire escape and lifted himself onto the landing.

He raised a foot to kick the window in, but Ronnie cautioned, "Open!" remembering Seamus' story about the actor who'd sneaked in to retrieve his wallet. Damen bent to the window and tried it. It slid smoothly upward, letting the odors of the loft waft toward him: dust, old fabric, and grease paint.

"Here!" Ronnie called out to Seamus. Damen echoed her thought, but softly, in case Spellman was holding Christy prisoner inside. "Christy, I'm here. Where are you?"

SEAMUS HEARD RONNIE'S CALL, but he was too busy trying to distract Kim to answer. He shouted, jiggled, and whistled in attempts to slow her down. When that didn't work, he tried to change her mind. "Run!" he encouraged. "Run!"

Kim was undeterred. Backing up the stairs, she moved along the railing to where she'd tied the rope to the banister and pulled up the loose end. Taking a scarf from the crate she'd brought out earlier, she tied it around the noose at the bottom. A few inches farther up, she tied a second scarf, repeating the process several times until pieces of light fabric lined the rope like ribbons on a kite string. At the base of the balcony rail, she stuffed the rest of the scarves between the uprights.

Reaching into her pocket, Kim pulled out her lighter, touched the flame to the scarf, and dropped the rope over the rail. As she hurried down the metal stairs, watching the back door for signs of anyone near it, the small ball of fire at the bottom of the rope burned merrily, tongues of flame reaching up toward the next scarf, where the process would continue until flames reached the bunched fabric and the old wooden floor.

At the bottom of the steps, Kim said softly into the darkness, "It won't matter if you stay and burn, Miss Parker, or try to get out the back door. Either way, you're dead."

CHRISTY HUDDLED behind the Victorian couch, trying to keep perfectly still and blend with the humps and bumps of scenery. When she heard Kim come down the stairs, she hugged her knees, taking no chance her upturned face would show as a lighter spot among the dark fabrics and woods. Once she was sure Kim had passed, she chanced a look. Above her, the rope she'd climbed down was aflame, the fire licking its way up a succession of fabric pieces tied to it. At the moment it looked like a stage effect, a harmless spot of brightness, but that would change when the flames reached the wooden floor of the loft. She had to get up there and put the fire out before the whole theatre went up in flames. But that was exactly what Kim wanted. If Christy came out of hiding, she'd shoot her.

Albert said he'd called for help. Could she afford to wait, or would the fire spread so quickly she'd be forced from her hiding place and killed? Panic swelled in her chest, but she forced it back, knowing any decision made in terror wouldn't be the best one.

Manageable parts, she reminded herself. Break the problem down. First, where was Kim? Probably by the back door, which meant Christy couldn't climb the stairs without being seen. The only advantage for her was that Kim was on the other side of the cyclorama. She couldn't see the stage or the wings. The *EXIT* light over the door shone only a few feet, and beyond that was darkness. Christy could move around if she was quiet, but she had no way to get out of the building.

That wasn't true, she realized. There was the fire escape in the loft. If she could get back up there, she could put out the fire, leave by the fire escape, and meet the police when they arrived.

But how could she get up there? She looked around for something to climb, something that would raise her high enough to reach the flames and put them out. The sets offered nothing: Victorian furniture, flimsy walls, and low tables. Nothing sturdy enough to climb.

Then it came to her. The guillotine! It was tall, sturdy, and high enough that she'd be able to reach the ball of flame moving steadily toward the loft floor.

Leaving her hiding place, Christy moved silently through

the clutter until she came to the east wall. Reaching up, she unfastened the chains that held the set piece in place. Holding the guide rope as she'd seen Josh do, she lifted the wooden frame slightly to free it from the hooks that anchored it to the wall. She tried not to think about the fact that Kim had done the same thing as she waited for Cassie to cross the stage in the dark.

Christy didn't let the set swing free. Although it took all her strength to do it, she held the rope taut, letting the guillotine settle slowly onto center stage. It made a thump as it landed, and Kim said, "You can't get away!" Her voice sounded a little desperate, as if the waiting was getting on her nerves.

Looking up at the burning rope, Christy climbed quickly onto the set piece. She stepped onto the board that would have held the unhappy victim's head in place, and lifted herself up, stretching to reach the framework that held the fake blade in place. Her foot slipped for a moment, but she somehow located a protruding dowel that allowed her to reach the top board with one hand. She paused, wondering what Kim was making of the creaks and scuffs her climbing created. It wasn't in Kim's interest to leave her position beside the exit to investigate. Christy hoped Kim remembered that.

With a great effort, Christy pulled herself onto the thin boards that formed the top of the guillotine. They weren't meant to bear weight, so she placed her feet on the uprights, not the cross-pieces themselves. Slowly, carefully, she stood up, balancing precariously and hoping Kim didn't decide to shine her flashlight upward anytime soon. As long as Kim thought Christy was trapped on the stage floor, she was safe.

Standing atop the guillotine, Christy could reach the beam that supported the cyclorama. Eight inches wide and two inches thick, it bolted into the opposing walls and was further supported with chains attached to the ceiling every few feet. Grasping the cross-piece with both hands, she transferred her weight to it, swinging her legs upward and clambering clumsily but successfully onto its surface. Ignoring the half inch of dust that clung to her, she stood up on the beam, teetering and fearful as she thought about falling fifteen feet to the hard wooden floor.

Now she had a different worry. Kim could easily see her if she turned her light upward. She had to remain totally silent from this point on. Pushing fear away, Christy steadied herself by holding onto the nearest chain and reached out for the loft's wrought-iron railing. It was a few inches beyond her grasp.

SEAMUS WAS ALMOST AS EDGY AS HIS HOST, but for the opposite reason. They both knew Christy was out there somewhere. Kim had passed from having any sort of plan to reacting to events. If she detected movement, she was likely to shoot at it. He had to do something.

He heard soft but definite noises coming from behind the curtain and moving upward. Someone, it had to be Christy, was climbing. He knew Kim could hear it, since he was using her ears, but she was focused on guarding the door, sure that Christy would try to get past her somehow. While Seamus couldn't guess the method or even the reason for Christy's ascent, he was desperate to keep Kim from noticing.

What could he do—tell her not to look up? That was likely to accomplish the very thing he wanted to avoid.

It came to him: it was possible in any old building and

something almost anyone would react to. "Rat!" he said loudly. "Rat!"

Kim's action was exactly what he'd hoped for. She scuttled backward, pulling in a breath and turning her flashlight beam onto the floor in wild circles. His ruse only distracted her for a few seconds, but Seamus figured that whatever Christy was trying to accomplish, he'd given her the time she needed.

CHRISTY LOOKED DOWN, though she knew she shouldn't. Her one chance was to make the jump to the railing, clamber over it as fast as she could, and head for the fire escape. It was the jump that scared her. She might miss the railing and fall. She might catch the railing but be unable to pull herself over it and hang there, an easy target for Kim to shoot. Those thoughts almost overcame her courage, but she pushed them away. *Think of the barn*, she told herself. *Cassie always went first, but she's not here now. This time, you have to do it alone.*

Bending her knees, Christy let go of the chain and reached with both hands for the railing, straightening her legs to propel herself forward. She caught the rail with both hands and immediately pulled her feet up, getting one and a second later the other onto the lower rail. From there it was fairly easy to pull herself to safety on the other side.

She made noise; it was unavoidable. The flashlight beam shone upward, but it was too late. Christy was over the railing, tumbling to the floor with a stifled grunt.

Staying well back from the edge of the loft, Christy pulled the burning rope upward. It slid smoothly through the metal uprights, and she stomped on it until the fire was extinguished. As she did, Christy heard two things: a siren in the distance, and Kim's scream of fury. At first she thought Kim had seen what she'd done, but her words didn't match that thought. "Let me go!" Kim was saying. "Get your hands off me!" A single shot rang out, followed by a yelp of pain.

A great clatter followed, and Christy heard the progress of what seemed like several people across the area below. Whether two or half a dozen, none of them could see where they were going, so there was a lot of grunting and bumping. Running footsteps echoed in the theatre, followed by a terrible crash. At almost the same moment, the backstage lights came on. Albert Marle stood in the corner, his hand still on the switch. Kim was on the stage, limping toward the apron as fast as she could go. John Damen came behind her, catching up and grasping her arms from behind.

"Give it up, Kim," he said firmly. "Where's Christy?"

"I'm up here," Christy called.

John turned toward her. "Are you all right?"

There were a thousand possible answers to that question. *No. I'm scared. I'm terrified. I'm exhausted. I'm relieved. I'm horrified. I'm grief-stricken.* Instead of those, Christy said, "I'm fine."

John turned to Albert Marle. "And you, sir?"

"Never better." Albert wore a black dressing gown embroidered with gold Egyptian hieroglyphs, "Did she try to shoot you, Miss Parker?" he called to Christy.

"She did."

He brandished a lacy parasol that took a sharp turn halfway up its spine. "Then I'm glad I whacked her with this, even if it is bent beyond repair."

Christy made her way down the stairs, holding onto the railing as if she were ninety years old. Albert met her at the bottom and put an arm around her shoulders. "I'm so glad you're all right."

"You came just in time, Albert."

He seemed pleased. "I did, didn't I? I crept down from my apartment and onto the stage. As I slid around the curtains, I saw that one standing under the exit light, taking aim at your young man here as he came down the back stairs." He turned to John. "Sorry I took so long, but I had to find something dark and rather Mata Hari to wear."

Christy thought he looked more like Dustin Hoffman in drag but she said, "As always, Albert, your timing is perfect, and your outfit's impressive too."

He led her to the stage, where John was applying handcuffs to a scowling Kim. "I didn't see her back there in the dark," he said to Albert. "I owe you."

"A tiny interview where I can mention the Vic will pay me back nicely," Albert assured him, smoothing his hair as if in preparation for the event.

"I think I broke my toe on that damned thing," Kim complained, pointing at the guillotine. "I need a doctor."

"We'll take care of that after you're booked." Damen turned to Christy. "What happened tonight?"

She started to tell the story but was interrupted by the

arrival of officers from the 22nd Division, who took Kim into custody at Damen's recommendation. Damen, Marle, and Christy agreed to come to the station house to explain recent events, so the story-telling was delayed.

That didn't matter to Christy. What mattered was John Damen's arm around her shoulders and his promise to stay with her as long as she wanted him to. It made her believe that everything was going to get better, not right away, of course, but someday.

IT WAS A LONG TIME before their hosts slept that night. Seamus waited until Damen's breathing slowed before saying, "I guess your case is closed, Ronnie."

"Yours too. Do you think your Ms. Parker will be convinced by what you found out?"

"Hard to say. She was pretty determined."

"We all fight it at first. You don't want to accept the fact that you're really done with Life, you know?"

"I know." His tone hinted he might still be dealing with that fact. "Do you think we could meet? Back on the ship?" He rushed to fill the silence that followed. "I don't mean anything by it, you know? But it was nice to have someone to talk to these last few days, someone who understands what it's like and why I do what I do."

Ronnie still didn't answer, and he felt a sinking dread. Finally she said, "Can you give me a little while to get ready? When I chose my outfit for this trip, I didn't expect to meet anybody, you know?"

Having worn the same suit for—well, for a very long time, Seamus didn't know, but he thought it was a good thing for a person to get spruced up to meet another person. Maybe he'd see if they had something for him at Raiment. Not a completely different suit, of course. Maybe the same thing in navy.

Other Books by Peg Herring

The Dead Detective Mysteries

The Dead Detective Agency

Dead for the Money

The Loser Mystery Series

Killing Silence

Killing Memories

Killing Despair

The Simon & Elizabeth Historical Mysteries

Her Highness' First Murder

Poison, Your Grace

The Lady Flirts with Death

Her Majesty's Mischief

Writing as Maggie Pill

The Sleuth Sisters

3 Sleuths, 2 Dogs, 1 Murder

Murder in the Boonies

About the Author

Peg Herring lives in Michigan with her husband of many years, but they often take to the road, looking for things they haven't seen yet. Visit her at http://pegherring.com

The next book of the Dead Detective Mysteries, *Dead to Get Ready—and Go,* will release in 2016.

Bored with life on the ship, Seamus decides it's time to do what he's been avoiding for six decades (Earth Time). Though he knows his wife and best friend teamed up to murder him, there are things about the crime he doesn't understand, as well as emotions he hasn't yet been able to face. With fellow Dead Detective Ronnie to assist him, Seamus returns to 1952 to face his memories and answer remaining questions about his death.

In a world much different from todays', in an America where questions of race and social justice are just beginning to be addressed, the two detectives find lots going on under the surface. Chicago offers opportunities for crime on many levels, and there's always someone around to take advantage of those with secrets. Seamus learns a shocking truth about his wife and the secret she kept from him, one that eventually led to his murder. In the end he and Ronnie must work to save the lives of two young cops brave enough—maybe foolhardy enough—to try to discover what really happened the night Seamus Hanrahan died.